WALK TWO MOONS

BY SHARON CREECH

HarperCollins*Publishers*

Walk Two Moons

Copyright © 1994 by Sharon Creech

ISBN 978-0-06-201444-3

Typography by Alicia Mikles

10 11 12 13 14 SCP 10 9 8 7 6 5 4 3 2 1

For my sister and brothers:
Sandy, Dennis, Doug, Tom
with love
from
The Favorite

DON'T JUDGE A MAN UNTIL YOU'VE WALKED
TWO MOONS IN HIS MOCCASINS.

Contents

1
A FACE AT THE WINDOW

GRAMPS SAYS THAT I AM A COUNTRY GIRL AT HEART, and that is true. I have lived most of my thirteen years in Bybanks, Kentucky, which is not much more than a caboodle of houses roosting in a green spot alongside the Ohio River. Just over a year ago, my father plucked me up like a weed and took me and all our belongings (no, that is not true—he did not bring the chestnut tree, the willow, the maple, the hayloft, or the swimming hole, which all belonged to me) and we drove three hundred miles straight north and stopped in front of a house in Euclid, Ohio.

"No trees?" I said. "This is where we're going to live?"

"No," my father said. "This is Margaret's house."

The front door of the house opened and a lady with wild red hair stood there. I looked up and down the street. The houses were all jammed together like a row of birdhouses. In front of each house was a tiny square of grass, and in front of that was a thin gray sidewalk running alongside a gray road.

"Where's the barn?" I asked. "The river? The swimming hole?"

"Oh, Sal," my father said. "Come on. There's Margaret." He waved to the lady at the door.

"We have to go back. I forgot something."

The lady with the wild red hair opened the door and came out onto the porch.

"In the back of my closet," I said, "under the floorboards. I put something there, and I've got to have it."

"Don't be a goose. Come and see Margaret."

I did not want to see Margaret. I stood there, looking around, and that's when I saw the face pressed up against an upstairs window next door. It was a round girl's face, and it looked afraid. I didn't know it then, but that face belonged to Phoebe Winterbottom, a girl who had a powerful imagination, who would become my friend, and who would have many peculiar things happen to her.

Not long ago, when I was locked in a car with my grandparents for six days, I told them the story of Phoebe, and when I finished telling them—or maybe even as I was telling them—I realized that the story of Phoebe was like the plaster wall in our old house in Bybanks, Kentucky.

My father started chipping away at a plaster wall in the living room of our house in Bybanks shortly after my mother left us one April morning. Our house was an old farmhouse that my parents had been restoring, room by room. Each night as he waited to hear from my mother, he chipped away at that wall.

On the night that we got the bad news—that she was not returning—he pounded and pounded on that wall with a chisel and a hammer. At two o'clock in the morning, he came up to my room. I was not asleep. He led me downstairs and showed me what he had found. Hidden behind the wall was a brick fireplace.

The reason that Phoebe's story reminds me of that plaster wall and the hidden fireplace is that beneath Phoebe's story was another one. Mine.

2
THE CHICKABIDDY
STARTS A STORY

IT WAS AFTER ALL THE ADVENTURES OF PHOEBE that my grandparents came up with a plan to drive from Kentucky to Ohio, where they would pick me up, and then the three of us would drive two thousand miles west to Lewiston, Idaho. This is how I came to be locked in a car with them for nearly a week. It was not a trip that I was eager to take, but it was one I had to take.

Gramps had said, "We'll see the whole ding-dong country!"

Gram squeezed my cheeks and said, "This trip will give me a chance to be with my favorite chickabiddy again." I am, by the way, their *only* chickabiddy.

My father said that Gram couldn't read maps worth a hill of beans, and that he was grateful that I had agreed to go along and help them find their way. I was only thirteen, and although I did have a way with maps, it was not really because of that skill that I was going, nor was it to see the "whole ding-dong country" that Gram and Gramps were going. The real reasons were buried beneath piles and piles of unsaid things.

Some of the real reasons were:

1. Gram and Gramps wanted to see Momma, who was resting peacefully in Lewiston, Idaho.
2. Gram and Gramps knew that I wanted to see Momma, but that I was afraid to.
3. Dad wanted to be alone with the red-headed Margaret Cadaver. He had already seen Momma, and he had not taken me.

Also—although this wasn't as important—Dad did not trust Gram and Gramps to behave themselves along the way unless they had me with them. Dad said that if they tried to go on their own, he would save everyone a lot of time and embarrassment by calling the police and having them arrested before they even left the driveway. It might sound a bit extreme for a man to call the police on his own tottery old parents, but when my grandparents got in a car, trouble just naturally followed them like a filly trailing behind a mare.

My grandparents Hiddle were my father's parents, full up to the tops of their heads with goodness and sweetness, and mixed in with all that goodness and sweetness was a large dash of peculiarity. This combination made them interesting to know, but you could never predict what they would do or say.

Once it was settled that the three of us would go, the journey took on an alarming, expanding need to hurry that was like a walloping great thundercloud assembling around me. During the week before we left, the sound of the wind was *hurry, hurry, hurry*, and at night even the silent darkness whispered *rush, rush, rush*. I did not think we would ever leave, and yet I did not want to leave. I did not really expect to survive the trip.

But I had decided to go and I would go, and I had to be there by my mother's birthday. This was extremely important. I believed that if there was any chance to bring my mother back home it would happen on her birthday. If I had said this aloud to my father or to my grandparents, they would have said that I might as well try to catch a fish in the air, so I did not say it aloud. But I believed it. Sometimes I am as ornery and stubborn as an old donkey. My father says I lean on broken reeds and will get a face full of swamp mud one day.

When at last Gram and Gramps Hiddle and I set out that first day of the trip, I prayed for the first thirty minutes solid. I prayed that we would not be in an accident (I was terrified of cars and buses) and that we would get there by my mother's birthday—seven days away—and that we would bring her home. Over and over, I prayed the same thing. I prayed to trees. This was easier than praying directly to God. There was nearly always a tree nearby.

As we pulled onto the Ohio Turnpike, which is the flattest, straightest piece of road in God's whole creation, Gram interrupted my prayers. "Salamanca—"

I should explain right off that my real name is Salamanca Tree Hiddle. Salamanca, my parents thought, was the name of the Indian tribe to which my great-great-grandmother belonged. My parents were mistaken. The name of the tribe was Seneca, but since my parents did not discover their error until after I was born and they were, by then, used to my name, it remained Salamanca.

My middle name, Tree, comes from your basic

tree, a thing of such beauty to my mother that she made it part of my name. She wanted to be more specific and use Sugar Maple Tree, her very favorite, but Salamanca Sugar Maple Tree Hiddle was a bit much even for her.

My mother used to call me Salamanca, but after she left, only my grandparents Hiddle called me Salamanca (when they were not calling me chickabiddy). To most other people, I was Sal, and to a few boys who thought they were especially amusing, I was Salamander.

In the car, as we started our long journey to Lewiston, Idaho, my grandmother Hiddle said, "Salamanca, why don't you entertain us?"

"What sort of thing did you have in mind?"

Gramps said, "How about a story? Spin us a yarn."

I certainly do know heaps of stories, but I learned most of them from Gramps. Gram suggested I tell one about my mother. That I could not do. I had just reached the point where I could stop thinking about her every minute of every day.

Gramps said, "Well then, what about your friends? You got any tales to tell about them?"

Instantly, Phoebe Winterbottom came to mind. There was certainly a hog's belly full of things to tell about her. "I could tell you an extensively strange story," I warned.

"Oh, good!" Gram said. "Delicious!"

And that is how I happened to suspend my tree prayers and tell them about Phoebe Winterbottom, her disappearing mother, and the lunatic.

3
BRAVERY

BECAUSE I FIRST SAW PHOEBE ON THE DAY MY father and I moved to Euclid, I began my story of Phoebe with the visit to the red-headed Margaret Cadaver's, where I also met Mrs. Partridge, her elderly mother. Margaret nearly fell over herself being nice to me. "What lovely hair," she said, and "Aren't you sweet!" I was *not* sweet that day. I was being particularly ornery. I wouldn't sit down and I wouldn't look at Margaret.

As we were leaving, Margaret whispered to my father, "John, have you told her yet—how we met?"

My father looked uncomfortable. "No," he said. "I tried—but she doesn't want to know."

Now that was the truth, absolutely. Who cares? I thought. Who cares how he met Margaret Cadaver?

When at last we left Mrs. Cadaver and Mrs.

Partridge, we drove for approximately three minutes. Two blocks from Margaret Cadaver's was the place where my father and I were now going to live.

Tiny, squirt trees. Little birdhouses in a row—and one of those birdhouses was ours. No swimming hole, no barn, no cows, no chickens, no pigs. Instead, a little white house with a miniature patch of green grass in front of it. It wasn't enough grass to keep a cow alive for five minutes.

"Let's take a tour," my father said, rather too heartily.

We walked through the tiny living room into the miniature kitchen and upstairs into my father's pint-sized bedroom and on into my pocket-sized bedroom and into the wee bathroom. I looked out the upstairs window down into the backyard. Half of the tiny yard was a cement patio and the other half was another patch of grass that our imaginary cow would devour in two bites. There was a tall wooden fence all around the yard, and to the left and right of our yard were other, identical fenced plots.

After the moving van arrived and two men crammed our Bybanks furniture into our birdhouse, my father and I inched into the living room, crawling over sofas and chairs and tables and boxes, boxes, boxes. "Mm," my father said. "It looks as if we tried to squeeze all the animals into the chicken coop."

Three days later, I started school and saw Phoebe again. She was in my class. Most of the kids in my new school spoke in quick, sharp bursts and dressed in stiff, new clothes and wore braces on their teeth. Most girls wore their hair in exactly the same way: in a shoulder-length "bob" (that's what they called it) with long bangs that they repeatedly shook out of their eyes. We once had a horse who did that.

Everybody kept touching my hair. "Don't you ever cut it?" they said. "Can you sit on it? How do you wash it? Is it naturally black like that? Do you use conditioner?" I couldn't tell if they liked my hair or if they thought I looked like a whangdoodle.

One girl, Mary Lou Finney, said the most peculiar things, like out of the blue she would say, "Omnipotent!" or "Beef brain!" I couldn't make any sense of it. There were Megan and Christy, who jumped up and down like parched peas, moody Beth Ann, and pink-cheeked Alex. There was Ben, who drew cartoons all day long, and a peculiar

English teacher named Mr. Birkway.

And then there was Phoebe Winterbottom. Ben called her "Free Bee Ice Bottom" and drew a picture of a bumblebee with an ice cube on its bottom. Phoebe tore it up.

Phoebe was a quiet girl who stayed mostly by herself. She had a pleasant round face and huge, enormous sky-blue eyes. Around this pleasant round face, her hair—as yellow as a crow's foot—curled in short ringlets.

During that first week, when my father and I were at Margaret's (we ate dinner there three times that week), I saw Phoebe's face twice more at her window. Once I waved at her, but she didn't seem to notice, and at school she never mentioned that she had seen me.

Then one day at lunch, she slid into the seat next to me and said, "Sal, you're so courageous. You're ever so brave."

To tell you the truth, I was surprised. You could have knocked me over with a chicken feather. "Me? I'm not brave," I said.

"You are. You are brave."

I was not. I, Salamanca Tree Hiddle, was afraid of lots and lots of things. For example, I was terrified of car accidents, death, cancer, brain tumors, nuclear war, pregnant women, loud noises, strict teachers, elevators, and scads of other things. But I was not afraid of spiders, snakes, and wasps. Phoebe, and nearly everyone else in my new class, did not have much fondness for these creatures.

But on that day, when a dignified black spider was investigating my desk, I cupped my hands around it, carried it to the open window, and set it outside on the ledge. Mary Lou Finney said, "Alpha and Omega, will you look at that!" Beth Ann was as white as milk. All around the room, people were acting as if I had singlehandedly taken on a fire-breathing dragon.

What I have since realized is that if people expect you to be brave, sometimes you pretend that you are, even when you are frightened down to your very bones. But this was later, during the whole thing with Phoebe's lunatic, that I realized this.

At this point in my story, Gram interrupted me to say, "Why, Salamanca, of course you're brave. All the Hiddles are brave. It's a family trait. Look at your daddy—your momma—"

"Momma's not a real Hiddle," I said.

"She practically is," Gram said. "You can't be married to a Hiddle that long and not *become* a Hiddle."

That is not what my mother used to say. She would tell my father, "You Hiddles are a mystery to me. I'll never be a true Hiddle." She did not say this proudly. She said it as if she were sorry about it, as if it were some sort of failing in her.

My mother's parents—my other set of grandparents—are Pickfords, and they are as unlike my grandparents Hiddle as a donkey is unlike a pickle. Grandmother and Grandfather Pickford stand straight up, as if sturdy, steel poles ran down their backs. They wear starched, ironed clothing, and when they are shocked or surprised (which is often), they say, "Really? Is that so?" and their eyes open wide and their mouths turn down at the corners.

Once I asked my mother why Grandmother and Grandfather Pickford never laughed. My mother said, "They're just so busy being respectable. It takes a lot of concentration to be that respectable." And then my mother laughed and laughed, in a gentle way, and you could tell her own spine was not made of steel because she bent in half, laughing and laughing.

My mother said that Grandmother Pickford's one act of defiance in her whole life as a Pickford was in naming her. Grandmother Pickford, whose own name is Gayfeather, named my mother Chan-hassen. It's an Indian name, meaning "tree sweet juice," or—in other words—maple sugar. Only Grandmother Pickford ever called my mother by her Indian name, though. Everyone else called my mother Sugar.

Most of the time, my mother seemed nothing like her parents at all, and it was hard for me to imagine that she had come from them. But occasionally, in small, unexpected moments, the corners of my mother's mouth would turn down and she'd say, "Really? Is that so?" and sound exactly like a Pickford.

4
THAT'S WHAT
I'M TELLING YOU

ON THE DAY THAT PHOEBE SAT NEXT TO ME AT lunch and told me I was brave, she invited me to her house for dinner. To be honest, I was relieved that I would not have to eat at Margaret's again. I did not want to see Dad and Margaret smiling at each other.

I wanted everything to be like it *was*. I wanted to be back in Bybanks, Kentucky, in the hills and the trees, near the cows and chickens and pigs. I wanted to run down the hill from the barn and through the kitchen door that banged behind me and see my mother and my father sitting at the table peeling apples.

Phoebe and I walked home from school to-gether. We stopped briefly at my house so that I could call my father at work. Margaret had helped him find a job selling farm machinery. He said it made him happy as a clam at high water to know I had a new friend. Maybe this is really why he was happy, I thought, or maybe it was because he could be alone with Margaret Cadaver.

Phoebe and I then walked to her house. As we passed Margaret Cadaver's house, a voice called out. "Sal? Sal? Is that you?"

In the shadows on the porch, Margaret's mother, Mrs. Partridge, sat in a wicker rocker. A thick, gnarled cane with a handle carved in the shape of a cobra's head lay across her knees. Her purple dress had slipped up over her bony knees, which were spread apart, and I hate to say it, but you could see right up her skirt. Around her neck was a yellow feather scarf. ("My boa," she once told me, "my most favoritest boa.")

As I started up the walk, Phoebe pulled on my arm. "Don't go up there," she said.

"It's only Mrs. Partridge," I said. "Come on."

"Who's that with you?" Mrs. Partridge said. "What's that on her face?" I knew what she was going to do. She did this with me the first time I met her.

Phoebe placed her hands on her own round face and felt about.

"Come here," Mrs. Partridge said. She wriggled

18

her crooked little fingers at Phoebe.

Mrs. Partridge put her fingers up to Phoebe's face and mashed around gently over her eyelids and down her cheeks. "Just as I thought. It's two eyes, a nose, and a mouth." Mrs. Partridge laughed a wicked laugh that sounded as if it were bouncing off jagged rocks. "You're thirteen years old."

"Yes," Phoebe said.

"I knew it," Mrs. Partridge said. "I just knew it." She patted her yellow feather boa.

"This is Phoebe Winterbottom," I said. "She lives right next door to you."

When we left, Phoebe whispered, "I wish you hadn't done that. I wish you hadn't told her I lived next door."

"Why not? You don't seem to know Mrs. Cadaver and Mrs. Partridge very well—"

"They haven't lived there very long. Only a month or so."

"Don't you think it's remarkable that she guessed your age?"

"I don't see what is so remarkable about it." Before I could explain, Phoebe started telling me about the time that she and her mother, father, and sister, Prudence, had gone to the State Fair. At one booth, a crowd was gathered around a tall, thin man.

"So what was he doing?" I asked.

"That's what I'm telling you," Phoebe said. Phoebe had a way of sounding like a grown-up sometimes. When she said, "That's what I'm telling you," she sounded like a grown-up talking to a child. "What he was doing was guessing people's ages. All around, people were saying, 'Oh!' and 'Amazing!' and 'How does he do that?' He had to guess your correct age within one year or else you won a teddy bear."

"How did he do it?" I asked.

"That's what I'm telling you," Phoebe said. "The thin man would look someone over carefully, close his eyes, and then he would point his finger at the person and shout, 'Seventy-two!'"

"At everyone? He guessed everyone to be seventy-two?"

"Sal," she said. "That's what I am trying to tell you. I was just giving an example. He might have said 'ten' or 'thirty' or—'seventy-two.' It just depended on the person. He was astounding."

I really thought it was more astounding that Mrs. Partridge could do this, but I didn't say anything.

Phoebe's father wanted the thin man to guess his age. "My father thinks he looks very young, and he was certain he could fool the man. After studying my father, the thin man closed his eyes, pointed his finger at my father and shouted, 'Fifty-two!' My father gave a little yelp, and all around people were automatically saying, 'Oh!' and 'Amazing' and all that. But my father stopped them."

"Why?"

Phoebe pulled on one of her yellow curls. I think she wished she hadn't started this story in the first place. "Because he wasn't anywhere near fifty-two. He was only thirty-eight."

"Oh."

"And all day long, my father followed us through the fair, carrying his prize, a large, green teddy bear. He was miserable. He kept saying, 'Fifty-two? *Fifty-two?* Do I look fifty-two?'"

"Does he?" I said.

Phoebe pulled harder on her hair. "No, he does not look fifty-two. He looks thirty-eight." She was very defensive about her father.

Phoebe's mother was in the kitchen. "I'm making blackberry pie," Mrs. Winterbottom said. "I hope you like blackberries—is there something wrong? Really, if you don't like blackberries, I could—"

"No," I said. "I like blackberries very much. I

just have some allergies, I think."

"To blackberries?" Mrs. Winterbottom said.

"No, not to blackberries." The truth is, I do not have allergies, but I could not admit that blackberries reminded me of my mother.

Mrs. Winterbottom made me and Phoebe sit down at the kitchen table and tell her about our day. Phoebe told her about Mrs. Partridge guessing her age.

"She's really remarkable," I said.

Phoebe said, "It's not *that* remarkable, Sal. I wouldn't exactly use the word *remarkable*."

"But Phoebe," I said. "Mrs. Partridge is blind."

Both Phoebe and her mother said, *"Blind?"*

Later, Phoebe said to me, "Don't you think it's odd that Mrs. Partridge, who is blind, could see something about me—but I, who can see, was blind about her? And speaking of odd, there's something very odd about that Mrs. Cadaver."

"Margaret?" I said.

"She scares me half to death," Phoebe said.

"Why?"

"That's what I'm telling you," she said. "First, there is that name: *Cadaver.* You know what cadaver means?"

Actually, I did not.

"It means *dead body*."

"Are you sure?" I said.

"Of course I'm sure, Sal. You can check the dictionary if you want. Do you know what she does for a living—what her job is?"

"Yes," I was pleased to say. I was pleased to know *something*. "She's a nurse."

"Exactly," Phoebe said. "Would you want a nurse whose name meant *dead body*? And that hair—don't you think all that sticking-out red hair is *spooky*? And that voice—it reminds me of dead leaves all blowing around on the ground."

This was Phoebe's power. In her world, no one was ordinary. People were either perfect—like her father—or, more often, they were lunatics or axe murderers. She could convince me of just about anything—especially about Margaret Cadaver. From that day on, Margaret Cadaver's hair did look spooky and her voice did sound exactly like dead leaves. Somehow it was easier to deal with Margaret if there were *reasons* not to like her, and I definitely did not want to like her.

"Do you want to know an absolute secret?" Phoebe said. (I did.) "Promise not to tell." (I promised.) "Maybe I shouldn't," she said. "Your father goes over there all the time. He likes her, doesn't he?" She twirled her finger through her curly hair and let those big blue eyes roam over the ceiling. "Her name is *Mrs.* Cadaver, right? Have you ever wondered what happened to *Mr.* Cadaver?"

"I never really thought about—"

"Well, I think I know," Phoebe said, "and it is awful, purely awful."

5

A DAMSEL IN DISTRESS

AT THIS POINT IN MY STORY ABOUT PHOEBE, GRAM said, "I knew somebody like Peeby once."

"*Phoebe*," I said.

"Yes, that's right. I knew someone just like Peeby, only her name was Gloria. Gloria lived in the wildest, most pepped-up world—a scary one, but oh!—scads more exciting than my own."

Gramps said, "Gloria? Is she the one who told you not to marry me? Is she the one who said I would be your ruination?"

"Shoosh," Gram said. "Gloria was right about that at least." She elbowed Gramps. "Besides, Gloria only said that because she wanted you for herself."

"Gol-dang!" Gramps said, pulling into a rest stop along the Ohio Turnpike. "I'm tired."

I did not want to stop. *Rush, rush, rush* whispered the wind, the sky, the clouds, the trees. *Rush, rush, rush.*

If all he wanted to do was take a rest, that seemed a safe enough and quick enough thing for him to do. My grandparents can get into trouble as easily as a fly can land on a watermelon.

Two years ago when they drove to Washington, D.C., they were arrested for stealing the back tires off a senator's car. "We had two flat, sprunkled tires," my grandfather explained. "We were only *borrowing* the senator's tires. We were going to return them." In Bybanks, Kentucky, you could do this. You could borrow someone's back tires and return them later, but you could not do this in Washington, D.C., and you could especially not do this to a senator's car.

Last year when Gram and Gramps drove to Philadelphia, they were stopped by the police for irresponsible driving. "You were driving on the shoulder," a policeman told Gramps. Gramps said, "Shoulder? I thought it was an extra lane. That's a mighty fine shoulder."

So here we were, just a few hours into our trip out to Lewiston, Idaho, and we were safely stopped in a rest area. Then Gramps noticed a woman leaning over the fender of her car. The woman was peering at her engine and dabbing a white handkerchief at various greasy items inside.

"Excuse me," Gramps said gallantly. "I believe I see a damsel in some distress," and off he marched to her rescue.

Gram sat there patting her knees and singing, "Oh meet me, in the tulips, when the tulips do bloooom—"

The woman's white handkerchief, now spotted with black grease, dangled from her fingertips as she smiled down on the back of Gramps, who had taken her place leaning over the engine.

"Might be the car-bust-er-ator," he said, "or maybe not." He tapped a few hoses. "Might be these dang snakes," he said.

"Oh my," the woman said. "Snakes? In my engine?"

Gramps waggled a hose. "This here is what I call a snake," he said.

"Oh, I see," the woman said. "And you think those—those snakes might be the problem?"

"Maybe so." Gramps pulled on one and it came loose. "See there?" he said. "It's off."

"Well, yes, but you—"

"Dang snakes," Gramps said, pulling at another one. It came loose. "Lookee there, another one."

The woman smiled a thin, little, worried smile. "But—"

Two hours later, there was not a single "snake" still attached to anything to which it was supposed to be attached. The "car-bust-erator" lay dismantled on the ground. Various other pieces of the woman's engine were scattered here and there.

The woman called a mechanic, and once Gramps was satisfied that the mechanic was an honest man who might actually be able to repair her car, we started on our trip again.

"Salamanca," Gram said, "tell us more about Peeby."

"Phoebe," I said. "Phoebe Winterbottom."

"Yes, that's right," Gram said. "Peeby."

6
BLACKBERRIES

"WHAT WAS THE DIABOLIC THING THAT HAPPENED to Mr. Cadaver?" Gramps asked. "You didn't tell us that yet."

I explained that just as Phoebe was going to divulge the purely awful thing that had happened to Mr. Cadaver, her father came home from work and we all sat down to dinner: me, Phoebe, Mr. and Mrs. Winterbottom, and Phoebe's sister, Prudence.

Phoebe's parents reminded me a lot of my other grandparents—the Pickfords. Like the Pickfords, Mr. and Mrs. Winterbottom spoke quietly, in short sentences, and sat straight up as they ate their food. They were extremely polite to each other, saying "Yes, Norma," and "Yes, George," and "Would you please pass the potatoes, Phoebe?" and "Wouldn't your guest like another helping?"

They were picky about their food. Everything they ate was what my father would call "side dishes": potatoes, zucchini, bean salad, and a mystery casserole that I could not identify. They didn't eat meat, and they didn't use butter. They were very much concerned with cholesterol.

From what I could gather, Mr. Winterbottom worked in an office, creating road maps. Mrs. Winterbottom baked and cleaned and did laundry and grocery shopping. I had a funny feeling that Mrs. Winterbottom did not actually like all this baking and cleaning and laundry and shopping, and I'm not quite sure why I had that feeling because if you just listened to the *words* she said, it sounded as if she was Mrs. Supreme Housewife.

For example, at one point Mrs. Winterbottom said, "I believe I've made more pies in the past week than I can count." She said this in a cheery voice, but afterward, in the small silence, when no one commented on her pies, she gave a soft sigh and looked down at her plate. I thought it was odd that she baked all those pies when she seemed so concerned about cholesterol.

A little later, she said, "I couldn't find exactly that brand of muesli you like so much, George, but I bought something similar." Mr. Winterbottom kept eating, and again, in that silence, Mrs. Winterbottom sighed and examined her plate.

I was happy for her when she announced that since Phoebe and Prudence were back in school, she thought she would return to work. Apparently, during the school terms she worked part-time at Rocky's Rubber as a receptionist. When no one commented on her going back to work, she sighed again and poked her potatoes.

A few times, Mrs. Winterbottom called her husband "sweetie pie" and "honey bun." She said, "Would you like more zucchini, sweetie pie?" and "Did I make enough potatoes, honey bun?"

For some reason that surprised me, those little names she used. She was dressed in a plain brown skirt and white blouse. On her feet were sensible, wide, flat shoes. She did not wear makeup. Even though she had a pleasant, round face and long, curly yellow hair, the main impression I got was that she was used to being plain and ordinary, that she was not supposed to do anything too shocking.

And Mr. Winterbottom was playing the role of Father, with a capital *F*. He sat at the head of the table with his white shirt cuffs rolled back neatly. He still wore his red-and-blue–striped tie. His expression was serious, his voice was deep, and his words were clear. "Yes, Norma," he said, deeply and clearly. "No, Norma." He looked more like fifty-two than thirty-eight, but this was not something I would ever call to his—or Phoebe's—attention.

Phoebe's sister, Prudence, was seventeen years old, but she acted like her mother. She ate primly, she nodded politely, she smiled after everything she said.

It all seemed peculiar. They acted so thumpingly *tidy* and *respectable*.

After dinner, Phoebe walked me home. She said, "You wouldn't think it to look at her, but Mrs. Cadaver is as strong as an ox." Phoebe looked behind her, as if she expected someone to be following us. "I have seen her chop down trees and lug the remains clear across her backyard. Do you know what I think? I think maybe she killed Mr. Cadaver and chopped him up and buried him in the backyard."

"Phoebe!" I said.

"Well, I'm just telling you what I think, that's all."

That night, as I lay in bed, I thought about Mrs. Cadaver, and I wanted to believe that she was capable of killing her husband and chopping him into pieces and burying him in the backyard.

And then I started thinking about the blackberries, and I remembered a time my mother and I walked around the rims of the fields and pastures in Bybanks, picking blackberries. We did not pick from the bottom of the vine or from the top. The ones at the bottom were for the rabbits, my mother said, and the ones at the top were for the birds. The ones at people-height were for people.

Lying in bed, remembering those blackberries, made me think of something else too. It was something that happened a couple years ago, on a morning when my mother slept late. It was that time she was pregnant. My father had already eaten breakfast, and he was out in the fields. On the table, my father had left a single flower in each of two juice glasses—a black-eyed susan in front of my place, and a white petunia in front of my mother's.

When my mother came into the kitchen that day, she said, "Glory!" She bent her face toward each flower. "Let's go find him."

We climbed the hill to the barn, crawled between the fence wires, and crossed the field. My father was standing at the far end of the field, his back to us, hands on his hips, looking at a section of fence.

My mother slowed down when she saw him. I was right behind her. It looked as if she wanted to creep up and surprise him, so I was quiet too and cautious in my steps. I could hardly keep from giggling. It seemed so daring to be sneaking up on my father, and I was sure my mother was going to throw her arms around him and kiss him and hug him and tell him how much she loved the flower on the kitchen table. My mother always loved anything that normally grows or lives out of doors—*anything*—lizards, trees, cows, caterpillars, birds, flowers, crickets, toads, ants, pigs.

Just before we reached my father, he turned around. This startled my mother and threw her off guard. She stopped.

"Sugar—" he said.

My mother opened her mouth, and I was thinking, "Come on! Throw your arms around him! Tell him!" But before she could speak, my father pointed to the fence and said, "Look at that. A morning's work." He indicated a new length of wire strung between two new posts. There was sweat on his face and arms.

And then I saw that my mother was crying. My father saw it too. "What—" he said.

"Oh, you're too *good*, John," she said. "You're too *good*. All you Hiddles are too good. I'll never be so good. I'll never be able to think of all the things—"

My father looked down at me. "The flowers," I said.

"Oh." He put his sweaty arms around her, but she was still crying and it wasn't what I had imagined it would be. It was all sad instead of happy.

The next morning when I went into the kitchen, my father was standing beside the table looking at two small dishes of blackberries—still shiny and wet with dew—one dish at his place and one at mine. "Thanks," I said.

"No, it wasn't me," he said. "It was your mother."

Just then, she came in from the back porch. My father put his arms around her and they smooched and it was all tremendously romantic, and I started to turn away, but my mother caught my arm. She pulled me to her and said to me—though it was meant for my father, I think—"See? I'm *almost* as good as your father!" She said it in a shy way, laughing a little. I felt betrayed, but I didn't know why.

It is surprising all the things you remember just by eating a blackberry pie.

7

ILL-AH-NO-WAY

"WELL, LOOKEE HERE!" GRAMPS SHOUTED. "THE
Illinois state line!" He pronounced Illinois "Ill-ah-
no-way," exactly the way everyone in Bybanks,
Kentucky, pronounced it, and hearing that "Ill-ah-
no-way" made me suddenly homesick for Bybanks.

"What happened to Indiana?" Gram said.

"Why, you gooseberry," Gramps said. "That's
where we've been the past three hours, barreling
through Indiana. You've been listening to the story
of Peeby and plumb missed Indiana. Don't you remember Elkhart? We ate lunch in Elkhart. Don't
you remember South Bend? You took a pee in
South Bend. Why, you missed the entire Hoosier
state! You gooseberry." He thought this was very
funny.

Just then, the road curved (it actually *curved*—
this was a shock), and off to the right was a huge
jing-bang mass of water. It was as blue as the blue-

bells that grow behind the barn in Bybanks, and that water just went on and on—it was all you could see. It looked like a huge blue pasture of water.

"Are we at the ocean?" Gram asked. "We're not supposed to be passing the ocean, are we?"

"You gooseberry, that's Lake Michigan." Gramps kissed his finger and put it against Gram's cheek.

"I sure would like to put my feet in that water," Gram said.

Gramps swerved across two lanes of traffic and onto the exit ramp, and faster than you could milk a cow we were standing barefoot in the cool water of Lake Michigan. The waves splashed up on our clothes, and the sea gulls flew in circles overhead, calling in one great chorus, as if they were glad to see us.

"Huzza, huzza!" Gram said, wriggling her heels into the sand. "Huzza, huzza!"

We stopped that night on the outskirts of Chicago. I looked around at what I could see of Ill-ah-no-way from the Howard Johnson Motel, and it might as well have been seven thousand miles from the lake. It all looked precisely like northern Ohio to me, with its flat land and long, straight roads, and I thought what a very long journey this was going to be. With the dark came the whispers: *rush, hurry, rush.*

That night I lay there trying to imagine Lewiston, Idaho, but my mind would not go forward to a place I had never been. Instead, I kept drifting back to Bybanks.

When my mother left for Lewiston, Idaho, that April, my first thoughts were, "How could she do that? How could she leave me?"

As the days went on, many things were harder and sadder, but some things were strangely easier. When my mother had been there, I was like a mirror. If she was happy, I was happy. If she was sad, I was sad. For the first few days after she left, I felt numb, non-feeling. I didn't know how to feel. I would find myself looking around for her, to see what I might want to feel.

One day, about two weeks after she had left, I was standing against the fence watching a newborn calf wobble on its thin legs. It tripped and wobbled and swung its big head in my direction and gave me a sweet, loving look. "Oh!" I thought. "I am happy at this moment in time." I was surprised that I knew this all by myself, without my mother there. And that night in bed, I did not cry. I said to myself, "Salamanca Tree Hiddle, you can be happy without her." It seemed a mean thought and I was sorry for it, but it *felt* true.

In the motel, as I was remembering these things, Gram came and sat on the edge of my bed. She said, "Do you miss your daddy? Do you want to call him?"

I did miss him, and I did want to call him, but I said, "No, I'm fine, really." He might think I was a goose if I had to call him already.

"Okay, then, chickabiddy," Gram said, and when she leaned over to kiss me, I could smell the baby powder she always used. That smell made me feel sad, but I didn't know why.

The next morning, when we got lost leaving Chicago, I prayed: "Please don't let us get in an accident, please get us there in time—"

Gramps said, "At least it's a mighty fine day for a drive." When we finally found a road heading west, we took it. Our plan was to curve across the lower part of Wisconsin, veer into Minnesota, and then barrel straight on through Minnesota, South Dakota, and Wyoming, sweep up into Montana, and cross the Rocky Mountains into Idaho. Gramps figured it would take us about a day in each state. He didn't intend to stop too much until we reached South Dakota, and he was really looking forward to South Dakota. "We're gonna see the Badlands," he said. "We're gonna see the Black Hills."

I didn't like the sound of either of those places, but I knew why we were going there. My mother had been there. The bus that she took out to Lewiston stopped in all the tourist spots. We were following along in her footsteps.

8
THE LUNATIC

ONCE WE WERE WELL ON THE ROAD OUT OF ILL-ah-no-way, Gram said, "Go on with Peeby. What happened next?"

"Do you want to hear about the lunatic?"

"Goodness!" Gram said, "as long as it's not too bloody. That Peeby is just like Gloria, I swear. A 'lunatic.' Imagine."

Gramps said, "Did Gloria really have a hankering for me?"

"Maybe she did, and maybe she didn't," Gram said.

"Well, gol-dang, I was only asking—"

"Seems to me," Gram said, "you've got enough to worry about, concentrating on these roads, without worrying about Gloria—"

Gramps winked at me in the rear-view mirror. "I think our gooseberry is jealous," he said.

"I am not," Gram said. "Tell about Peeby, chickabiddy."

I didn't want Gram and Gramps to get in a fight over Gloria, so I was happy to continue telling Phoebe's story.

I was at Phoebe's one Saturday morning when Mary Lou Finney called and invited us over to her house. Phoebe's parents were out, and Phoebe went all around the house checking to make sure that the doors and windows were locked. Her mother had already done this, but she made Phoebe promise to do it as well. "Just in case," Mrs. Winterbottom had said. I was not sure "just in case" of what—maybe in case someone had snuck in and opened all the windows and doors in the fifteen minutes between the time she left and the time we did. "You can never be *too* careful," Mrs. Winterbottom had said.

The doorbell rang. Phoebe and I looked out the window. Standing on the porch was a young man who looked about seventeen or eighteen, although I am not as good at guessing people's ages as blind Mrs. Partridge is. The young man was wearing a black T-shirt and blue jeans, and his hands were stuffed into his pockets. He seemed nervous.

"My mother hates it when strangers come to the door," Phoebe said. "She is convinced that any day one of them will burst into the house with a gun and turn out to be an escaped lunatic."

"Oh, honestly, Phoebe," I said. "Do you want me to answer the door?"

Phoebe took a deep breath. "We'll do it together." She opened the door and said hello in a cool voice.

"Is this 49 Gray Street?" the young man said.

"Yes," Phoebe said.

"So the Winterbottoms live here?"

After Phoebe admitted that yes, it was the Winterbottom residence, she said, "Excuse me a moment, please," and she closed the door. "Sal, do you detect any signs of lunacy? There doesn't appear to be any place he could be hiding a gun. His jeans are really tight. Maybe he has a knife tucked into his socks."

Phoebe could really be dramatic. "He isn't wearing any socks," I said. Phoebe opened the door again.

The young man said, "I want to see Mrs. Winterbottom. Is she here or what?"

"Yes," Phoebe lied.

The young man looked up and down the street. His hair was curly and mussed, and there were bright pink circles on his cheeks.

He wouldn't look us straight in the eye, but instead kept glancing to left and right. "I want to talk to her," he said.

"She can't come to the door right now," Phoebe said.

I thought he might actually cry when Phoebe said that. He chewed on his lip and blinked three or four times quickly. "I'll wait," he said.

"Just a minute," Phoebe said, closing the door. She pretended to look for her mother. "Mom!" she called. "Yoo-hoo!" She went upstairs, thumping loudly on the steps. "Mother!"

Phoebe and I returned to the door. He was still standing there with his hands in his pockets staring mournfully at Phoebe's house. "That's strange," Phoebe said to him. "I *thought* she was here, but she must have gone out. There's a whole lot of other people here though," she added quickly. "Scads and scads of people, but no Mrs. Winterbottom."

"Is Mrs. Winterbottom your mother?" he asked.

"Yes," Phoebe said. "Would you like me to leave a message?"

The little pink circles on his cheeks became even pinker. "No!" he said. "No. I don't think so. No." He looked up and down the street and then up at the number above the door. "What's your name?"

"Phoebe."

He repeated her name. "Phoebe Winterbottom." I thought he was going to make a joke about her name, but he didn't. He glanced at me. "Are you a Winterbottom too?" he asked.

"No," I said. "I'm a visitor."

And then he left. He just turned around, walked slowly down the porch steps and on down the street. We waited until he had turned the corner before we left. We ran all the way to Mary Lou's. Phoebe was certain that the young man was going to ambush us. Honestly. Like I said, she has a vivid imagination.

9
THE MESSAGE

ON THE WAY TO MARY LOU'S, PHOEBE SAID, "MARY Lou's family is not nearly as civilized as ours."

"In what way?" I asked.

"Oh, you'll see," Phoebe said.

Mary Lou Finney and Ben Finney were both in our class at school. At first I thought they were sister and brother, but Phoebe told me they were cousins, and that Ben was living with Mary Lou's family temporarily. Apparently there was always at least one stray relative living at the Finneys' temporarily.

It was complete pandemonium at the Finneys'. Mary Lou had an older sister and three brothers. In addition, there were her parents and Ben. There were footballs and basketballs lying all over the place, and boys sliding down the banister and leaping over tables and talking with their mouths full and interrupting everyone with endless questions. Phoebe took one look around and whispered to me, "Mary Lou's parents do not seem to have much control over things." Phoebe could sound a bit prissy sometimes.

Mr. Finney was lying in the bathtub, with all his clothes on, reading a book. From Mary Lou's bedroom window, I saw Mrs. Finney lying on top of the garage with a pillow under her head. "What's she doing?" I asked.

Mary Lou peered out the window. "King of kings! She's taking a nap."

When Mr. Finney got out of the bathtub, he went out in the backyard and tossed a football around with Dennis and Dougie, two of Mary Lou's brothers. Mr. Finney shouted, "Over here!" and "Thataway!" and "Way to go!"

The previous weekend, we had had a school sports day. Parents were watching their children show off, and there were even some events for the parents too, such as the three-legged race and pass-the-grapefruit. My father could not come, but Mary Lou's parents were there and so were Phoebe's.

Phoebe had said, "The games are a little childish sometimes, which is why my parents don't usually participate." Her parents stood on the sidelines while Mr. and Mrs. Finney ran around shouting "Over here!" and "Way-ta-go!" In the three-legged race, the Finneys kept falling over. Phoebe said, "I wonder if Mary Lou is embarrassed because of the way her parents are acting."

I didn't think it was embarrassing. I thought it was nice, but I didn't say so to Phoebe. I think that deep down Phoebe thought it was nice too, and she wished her own parents would act more like the Finneys. She couldn't admit this, though, and in a way, I liked this about Phoebe—that she tried to defend her family.

On the day that Phoebe and I met the potential lunatic and then went over to Mary Lou's, a couple other peculiar things happened. We were sitting on the floor of Mary Lou's room, and Phoebe was telling Mary Lou about the mysterious potential lunatic. Mary Lou's brothers, Dennis, Doug, and Tommy, kept dashing in and out of the room, leaping on the bed and squirting us with squirt guns.

Mary Lou's cousin Ben was lying on her bed, staring at me with his black, black eyes. They looked like two sparkly black discs set into big, round sockets. His dark eyelashes were long and feathery, casting shadows on his cheeks.

"I like your hair," he said to me. "Can you sit on it?"

"Yes, if I want."

Ben picked up a piece of paper from Mary Lou's desk, lay back down on the bed and drew a picture of a lizardlike creature with long black hair that, as it ran down the lizard's back and under its bottom, became a chair with legs. Underneath this, Ben had written, "Salamander sitting on her hair."

"Very amusing," Phoebe said. She left the room, and Mary Lou followed her.

I turned around to hand the drawing back to Ben, just as he leaned forward and mashed his lips into my collarbone. His lips rested there a moment. My nose was pressed into his hair, which smelled like grapefruit. Then he rolled off the bed, grabbed the drawing, and dashed out of the room.

Did he actually *kiss* my collarbone? And if he did, why did he do that? Was the kiss supposed to land somewhere else, like on my mouth, for example? That was a chilling thought. Had I imagined it? Maybe he merely brushed against me as he was rolling off the bed.

On the way home from Mary Lou's that day, Phoebe said, "Wasn't it, well, *loud* there?"

"I didn't mind," I said. I was thinking of something my father once said to my mother, "We'll fill the house up with children! We'll fill it right up to the brim!" But they hadn't filled it up. It was just me and them, and then it was just me and my father.

When we got back to Phoebe's house, her mother was lying on the couch, dabbing at her eyes with a tissue. "Is something wrong?" Phoebe asked.

"Oh no," Mrs. Winterbottom said. "Nothing's wrong."

Then Phoebe told her mother about the potential lunatic who had come to the house earlier. This news upset Mrs. Winterbottom. She wanted to know exactly what he had said and what Phoebe said and what he looked like and how he acted and how Phoebe acted, on and on. At last Mrs. Winterbottom said, "I think we had better not mention this to your father." She reached forward as if to hug Phoebe, but Phoebe pulled away.

Later Phoebe said, "That's odd. Usually my mother tells my father absolutely everything."

"Maybe she's just trying to save you from getting into trouble for talking with a stranger."

"I still don't like keeping it secret from him," Phoebe said.

We walked out onto her porch and there, lying on the top step was a white envelope. There was no name or anything on the outside. I thought it was one of those advertisements for painting your house or cleaning your carpets. Phoebe opened it. "Gosh," she said. Inside was a small piece of blue paper and on it was printed this message: *Don't judge a man until you've walked two moons in his moccasins.*

"What an odd thing," Phoebe said.

When Phoebe showed the message to her mother, Mrs. Winterbottom clutched at her collar. "Who could it be for?" Mrs. Winterbottom asked.

Mr. Winterbottom came in the back door, carrying his golf clubs. "Look, George," Mrs. Winterbottom said. "Who could this be for?"

"I couldn't say, really," Mr. Winterbottom said.

"But George, why would someone send us that message?"

"I couldn't say, Norma. Maybe it isn't for us."

"Not for us?" Mrs. Winterbottom said. "But it was on our steps."

"Really, Norma. It could be for anyone. Maybe it's for Prudence. Or Phoebe."

"Phoebe?" Mrs. Winterbottom asked. "Is it for you?"

"For me?" Phoebe said. "I don't think so."

"Well, who is it *for*?" Mrs. Winterbottom said. She was awfully worried. I believe she thought it came from the potential lunatic.

10
HUZZA, HUZZA

I HAD JUST FINISHED TELLING GRAM AND GRAMPS about the mysterious message when Gramps pulled off the freeway. He said he was tired of chewing up the road, and the white lines down the middle of the highway were starting to wiggle. As he drove into Madison, Wisconsin, Gram said, "I feel a little sorry for Mrs. Winterbottom. She doesn't sound very happy."

"They all sound screwy, if you ask me," Gramps said.

"Being a mother is like trying to hold a wolf by the ears," Gram said. "If you have three or four—or more—chickabiddies, you're dancing on a hot griddle all the time. You don't have time to think about anything else. And if you've only got one or two, it's almost harder. You have room left over—empty spaces that you think you've got to fill up."

"Well, it sure ain't a cinch being a father, either," Gramps said.

Gram touched his arm. "Horsefeathers," she said.

Round and round we drove until Gramps saw a parking space. Another car saw it too, but Gramps was fast and pulled in, and when the man in the other car waved his fist, Gramps said, "I'm a veteran. See this leg? Shrapnel from German guns. I saved our country!"

We did not have the correct change for the parking meter, so Gramps wrote a long note about how he was a visitor from Bybanks, Kentucky, and he was a World War II veteran with German shrapnel in his leg, and he kindly appreciated the members of the fair city of Madison allowing him to park in this space even though he did not have the correct change for the meter. He put this note on the dashboard.

"Do you really have German shrapnel in your leg?" I asked.

Gramps looked up at the sky. "Mighty nice day," he said.

The shrapnel was imaginary. Sometimes I am a little slow to figure these things out. My father once said I was as gullible as a fish. I thought he said *edible*. I thought he meant I was tasty.

The city of Madison sprawls between two lakes, Lake Mendota and Lake Monona, and dribbling out of these are other piddly lakes. It seemed as if the whole city was on vacation, with people riding around on their bikes and walking along the lakes and feeding the ducks and eating and canoeing and windsurfing. I'd never seen anything like it. Gram kept saying, "Huzza, huzza!"

There's a part of the city where no cars can go, and thousands of people stroll around eating ice cream. We went into Ella's Kosher Deli and Ice Cream Parlor and ate pastrami sandwiches and kosher dill pickles, followed by raspberry ice cream. After we walked around some more, we were hungry again, and so we had lemon tea and blueberry muffins at the Steep and Brew.

All the while, I heard the whispers: *rush, hurry, rush*. Gram and Gramps moved so slowly. "Shouldn't we go now?" I kept asking, but Gram would say, "Huzza, huzza!" and Gramps would say, "We'll go soon, chickabiddy, soon."

"Don't you want to send any postcards?" Gram asked.

"No, I do not."

"Not even to your daddy?"

"No." There was a good reason for this. All along her trip, my mother had sent me postcards. She wrote, "Here I am in the Badlands, missing you terribly," and "This is Mount Rushmore, but I don't see any Presidents' faces, I only see yours." The last postcard arrived two days after we found out she wasn't coming back. It was from Coeur d'Alene, Idaho. On the front was a picture of a beautiful blue lake surrounded by tall evergreens. On the back she had written, "Tomorrow I'll be in Lewiston. I love you, my Salamanca Tree."

At last, Gramps said, "I sure hate to get back on the road, but time's a-wastin'!"

Yes, I thought, yes, yes, yes!

Gram settled back for a nap while I said a few thousand more prayers. The next thing I knew, Gramps was pulling off the road again. "Lookee here," he said. "The Wisconsin Dells." He drove into a vast parking area and said, "Why don't you two go look around? I'm going to get a little shut-eye."

Gram and I poked our noses into an old fort, and then sat on the grass watching a group of Native Americans dance and beat drums. My mother had not liked the term *Native Americans*. She thought it sounded primitive and stiff. She said, "My great-grandmother was a Seneca Indian, and

I'm proud of it. She wasn't a Seneca Native American. *Indian* sounds much more brave and elegant." In school, our teacher told us we had to say Native American, but I agreed with my mother. *Indian* sounded much better. My mother and I liked this Indian-ness in our background. She said it made us appreciate the gifts of nature; it made us closer to the land.

I lay back and closed my eyes, listening to the drums beat *rush-rush-rush* and the dancers chant *hurry-hurry-hurry*. Someone was jingling bells, too, and for a moment I thought of Christmas and sleigh bells. When I opened my eyes again, Gram was gone.

I glanced around, trying to remember where we had parked the car. I looked through the crowd, back at the trees, over at the concession stand. "They've gone," I thought. "They've left me." I pushed through the people.

The crowd was clapping, the drums were beating. I was all turned around and could not remember which way we had come. There were three signs indicating different parking areas. The drums thundered. I pushed further into the crowd of people, who were now clapping louder, in time with the drums.

The Indians had formed two circles, one inside the other, and were hopping up and down. The men danced in the outer circle and wore feather headdresses and short leather aprons. On their feet were moccasins, and I thought again about Phoebe's message: *Don't judge a man until you've walked two moons in his moccasins.*

Inside the circle of men, the women in long dresses and ropes of beads had joined arms and were dancing around one older woman who was wearing a regular cotton dress. On her head was an enormous headdress, which had slipped down over her forehead.

I looked closer. The woman in the center was hopping up and down. On her feet were flat, white shoes. In the space between drum beats, I heard her say, "Huzza, huzza."

11
FLINCHING

EARLY THE NEXT MORNING, WE LEFT WISCONSIN and drove on, eating up the road through the lower rim of Minnesota. The land here was hilly and green, forests tucked in close beside the road, and the air smelled of pine.

"At last," Gramps said, "some scenery! I love a place that has scenery, don't you, chickabiddy?"

I had not said anything about what had happened the day before—about being scared down to my very bones when I thought they had left me. I don't know what came over me. Ever since my mother left us that April day, I suspected that everyone was going to leave, one by one.

I was glad to be able to go on with Phoebe's story, because when I was talking about Phoebe, I wasn't thinking about much else.

"Did Peeby get any more messages?" Gram asked.

⊂⊂

She did. The following Saturday, Phoebe and I were going to Mary Lou's again. As we left Phoebe's house, there on the front steps was another white envelope with a blue sheet of paper inside. The message was: *Everyone has his own agenda.*

Phoebe and I looked up and down the street. There was no sign of the message-leaver. Mary Lou thought the messages (this one and the other one) were intriguing. "How exciting!" she said. "I wish someone would leave *me* messages!"

Phoebe thought the messages were spooky. It was not the words that bothered her—nothing too frightening there—it was the idea that someone was sneaking around and leaving them on her porch. She worried that someone was watching their house, waiting for the right moment to leave the message. Phoebe was a champion worrier.

We tried to figure out what the message meant. "Okay," Phoebe said, "an agenda is a list of things to be discussed at a meeting—"

"So maybe it's for your dad," I suggested. "Does he go to meetings?"

"Well, I guess," Phoebe said. "He's ever so busy all day long."

"Maybe it's from his boss," Mary Lou said. "Maybe your father hasn't been conducting his meetings very well."

"My father is very organized," Phoebe said.

"What about the other message?" Mary Lou said. "Don't judge a man until you've walked two moons in his moccasins."

"I know what it means," I said. "I've heard my father use it lots of times. I used to imagine that there were two moons sitting in a pair of Indian shoes, but my father said it means that you shouldn't judge someone until you've walked in their moccasins. Until you've been in their shoes. In their place."

"And your father says this often?" Phoebe said.

"I know what you're thinking," I said, "but my father isn't creeping around leaving those messages. It isn't his handwriting."

When Ben came into Mary Lou's room, she asked him what he thought it meant. He took a sheet of paper from her desk and quickly drew a cartoon. It was a little spooky, because what he drew was identical to what I used to imagine: a pair of Indian moccasins with two moons in them.

"Maybe," Mary Lou said to Phoebe, "your father is being too quick to judge people at work. He needs to walk in their moccasins first."

"My father does *not* judge too quickly," Phoebe said.

"You don't have to get defensive," Ben said.

"I am not getting defensive. I'm just telling you that my father does not judge too quickly."

Later, we went to the drugstore. I thought it was going to be only me and Phoebe and Mary Lou going, but by the time we left the house, we had accumulated Tommy and Dougie as well. At the last minute, Ben said he was coming too.

"I don't know how you can stand it," Phoebe said to Mary Lou.

"Stand what?"

Phoebe pointed to Tommy and Dougie, who were running around like wound-up toys, making airplane noises and train noises and zooming in between us and then running up ahead and falling over each other and crying and then leaping back up again and socking each other and chasing after bumblebees.

"I'm used to it," Mary Lou said. "My brothers are always doing beef-brained things."

Ben walked right behind me all the way, which made me nervous. I kept turning around to see what he was doing back there, but he was just strolling along smiling.

Tommy bashed into me, and when I started to fall backward, Ben caught me. He put his arms around my waist and held on to me, even after it was obvious that I was not going to fall. I could smell that funny grapefruit smell again and feel his face pressed up against my hair. "Let go," I said, but he didn't let go. I had an odd sensation, as if a little creature was crawling up my spine. It wasn't a horrible sensation, more light and tickly. I thought maybe he dropped something down my shirt. "Let go!" I said, and finally he did.

It was at the drugstore that I got a little scared. Maybe I had been listening to Phoebe's tales of lunatics and axe murderers too much. Phoebe and I were looking at the magazines when I felt as if someone was watching us. I looked over to where Ben was standing, but he and Mary Lou were busy rummaging around in the chocolate bars. The feeling did not go away. I turned the other way around, and there on the far side of the store was the nervous young man who had come to Phoebe's house. He was at the cash register, paying for something, but he was staring at us while he was handing his money to the clerk. I nudged Phoebe. "Oh no," she said, "the lunatic." Phoebe hustled over to Ben and Mary Lou. "Look, quick, it's the lunatic."

"Where?"

"At the cash register."

"There's nobody there," Mary Lou said.

"Honest, he was there," Phoebe said. "I swear he was. Ask Sal."

"He was there," I said.

Later, when we had left Mary Lou and were on our way to Phoebe's house, we heard someone running up behind us. Phoebe thought we were doomed. "If we get our heads bashed in and that lunatic leaves us here on the sidewalk—" she said.

I felt a hand on my shoulder, and I opened my mouth to scream, but nothing came out. My brain was saying, "Scream! Scream!" but my voice was completely shut off.

It was Ben. He said, "Did I scare you?"

"That wasn't very funny," Phoebe said.

"I'll walk home with you," he said. "Just in case there are any—any—lunatics around." He had difficulty saying *lunatic*. On the way to Phoebe's house Ben said some odd things. First, he said, "Maybe you shouldn't call him a lunatic."

"And why not?" Phoebe said.

"Because a lunatic is—it means—it sounds like—oh, never mind." He would not explain, and he seemed embarrassed to have mentioned this in the first place. Then he said to me, "Don't people touch each other at your house?"

"What's that supposed to mean?"

"I just wondered," he said. "You flinch every time someone touches you."

"I do not."

"You do." He touched my arm. I have to admit, my instinct was to flinch but I caught myself. I pretended not to notice that his hand was resting there on my arm. That creature tickling my spine was back. "Hmm," he said, like a doctor examining a patient. "Hmm." He removed his hand. "Where's your mother?"

I had not mentioned my mother to anyone, not even Phoebe, except for the one time Phoebe had asked about her and I had only said she didn't live with us.

Ben said, "I saw your father once, but I've never seen your mother. Where is she?"

"She's in Idaho. Lewiston, Idaho."

"What's she doing there?" Ben said.

"I don't really feel like saying." It didn't occur to me to ask him where *his* mother was.

He touched my arm again. When I flinched, he said, "Ha! Gotcha!"

It bothered me, what he had said. It occurred to me that my father didn't hug me as much anymore, and that maybe I *was* starting to flinch whenever anyone touched me. I wasn't always like that. We used to be a hugging family. As I walked along with Ben and Phoebe, I remembered a time when I was nine or ten. My mother crawled into bed with me and snuggled close and said, "Let's build a raft and float away down a river." I used to think about that raft a lot, and I actually believed that one day we might build a raft and float away down a river together. But when she went to Lewiston, Idaho, she went alone.

Ben touched Phoebe's arm. She flinched. "Ha," he said. "Gotcha. You're jumpy, too, Free Bee."

And that, too, bothered me. I had already noticed how tense Phoebe's whole family seemed, how tidy, how respectable, how thumpingly *stiff*. Was I becoming like that? Why were they like that? A couple times I had seen Phoebe's mother try to touch Phoebe or Prudence or Mr. Winterbottom, but they all drew back from her. It was as if they had outgrown her.

Had I been drawing away from my own

mother? Did she have empty spaces left over? Was that why she left?

When we reached Phoebe's driveway, Ben said, "I guess you're safe now. I guess I'll go."

"Go ahead," Phoebe said.

Mrs. Cadaver came screeching up to the curb in her yellow Volkswagen, with her wild red witch hair flying all over the place. She waved at us and started pulling things out of the car and plopping them on the sidewalk.

"Who's that?" Ben asked.

"Mrs. Cadaver."

"Cadaver? Like dead body?"

"That's right."

"Hi, Sal," Mrs. Cadaver called. She dumped a pile of lumpy bags on the sidewalk. Ben asked if she wanted any help. "My, you're very polite," Mrs. Cadaver said, flashing her wild gray eyes.

"She scares me half to death," Phoebe said. "Don't go inside," she whispered to Ben.

"Why not?" he said, too loudly, because Mrs. Cadaver looked up and said, "What?"

"Oh nothing," Phoebe said.

Mrs. Cadaver said, "Sal, do you want to come in?"

"I was just going to Phoebe's," I said, glad for an excuse.

Phoebe's mother came to her front door. "Phoebe? What are you doing? Are you coming in?"

We left Ben. As we were going in Phoebe's house, we saw Ben lift something off the sidewalk. It was a shiny new axe.

Phoebe's mother said, "Is that Mary Lou's brother? Was he walking you home? Where's Mary Lou?"

"I hate it when you ask me three questions in a row," Phoebe said. Through the window, we could see Ben lugging the axe up the front steps of Mrs. Cadaver's house. Phoebe called out, "Don't go in!" but when Mrs. Cadaver held the front door open, Ben disappeared inside.

"Phoebe, what *are* you doing?" her mother asked.

Then Phoebe pulled the envelope out of her pocket, the envelope containing the newest message. "I found this outside," Phoebe said.

Mrs. Winterbottom opened the envelope carefully, as if it might contain a miniature bomb. "Oh sweetie," she said. "Who is it from? Who is it for? What does it mean?" Phoebe explained what an agenda was. "I know what an agenda is, Phoebe. I don't like this at all. I want to know who is sending these."

I was waiting for Phoebe to tell her about seeing the nervous young man at the drugstore, but Phoebe didn't mention it. A little later we saw Ben leave Mrs. Cadaver's house. He appeared to be all in one piece.

That day when I got home, my father was in the garage, tinkering with the car. He was leaning over the engine, and I couldn't see his face at first. "Dad—what do you think it means if someone touches someone else and the person being touched flinches? Do you think it means that the person being touched is getting too stiff?"

Dad turned slowly around. His eyes were red and puffy. I think he had been crying. His hands and shirt were greasy, but when he hugged me, I didn't flinch.

12
THE MARRIAGE BED

WHEN I HAD FIRST STARTED TELLING PHOEBE'S story, Gram and Gramps sat quietly and listened. Gramps concentrated on the road, and Gram gazed out the window. Occasionally, they interjected a "Gol-dang!" or a "No kidding?" But as I got farther into the story, they began to interrupt more and more.

When I told about the message *Everyone has his own agenda*, Gram thumped on the dashboard and said, "Isn't that the truth! Lordy! Isn't that what it is all about?"

I said, "How do you mean?"

"Everybody is just walking along concerned with his own problems, his own life, his own worries. And we're all expecting other people to tune into our own agenda. 'Look at my worry. Worry with me. Step into my life. Care about my problems. Care about me.'" Gram sighed.

Gramps scratched his head. "You turning into a philosopher or something?"

"Mind your own agenda," she said.

When I mentioned about Ben asking where my mother was and my saying that she was in Lewiston, but that I didn't want to elaborate, Gram and Gramps looked at each other. Gramps said, "One time my father took off for six months and didn't tell a soul where he was going. When my best friend asked me where my father was, I hauled off and punched him in the jaw. My best friend. I punched him dang in the jaw."

"You never told me that," Gram said. "I hope he socked you back."

Gramps pointed to a gap in his teeth. "See that? He knocked my tooth dang out."

And when I told Gram and Gramps about flinching when Ben touched me and about how I went home and found Dad in the garage, Gram unbuckled her seat belt, turned all the way around and leaned over the back of her seat. She took my hand and kissed it. Gramps said, "Give her one for me, too," and so Gram kissed my hand again.

Several times when I described Phoebe's world of lunatics and axe murderers, Gram said, "Just like Gloria, I swear to goodness. Just exactly like

Gloria." Once, after she said this, Gramps got a dreamy look on his face and Gram said, "Quit that mooning over Gloria. I know what you're thinking."

Gramps said, "Hear that, chickabiddy? This here gooseberry knows everything that runs through my head. Isn't she something?"

Just before we reached the South Dakota border, Gramps took a detour north because he had seen a sign advertising the Pipestone National Monument in Pipestone, Minnesota. On the sign was a picture of an Indian smoking a pipe.

"What do you want to go see an old Indian smoking a pipe for?" Gram asked. She didn't like the term *Native American* any more than my mother did.

"I just do," Gramps said. "We might not ever get the chance again."

"To see an Indian smoking a pipe?" Gram said.

"Will it take very long?" I asked as the air screamed, *hurry, hurry, hurry*.

"Not too long, chickabiddy. We've got to cool off our car-bust-er-ators. These roads are taking the poop out of me."

The detour to Pipestone wound through a cool, dark forest and if you closed your eyes and smelled the air, you could smell Bybanks, Kentucky.

Pipestone was a small town. Everywhere we went, people were talking to each other: standing there talking, or sitting on a bench talking, or walking along the street talking. When we passed by, they looked up at us, right into our faces and said "Hi" or "Howdy," and although it sounds corny to say it, we felt right at home there. It was so like Bybanks, where everyone you see stops to say something because they know you and have known you their whole lives.

We went to the Pipestone National Monument and saw Indians thunking away at the stone in the quarry. I asked one if he was a Native American, but he said, "No. I'm a person." I said, "But are you a Native American person?" He said, "No, I'm an American Indian person." I said, "So am I. In my blood."

We watched other American Indian persons making pipes out of the stone. In the Pipe Museum, we learned more about pipes than any human being ought to know. In a little clearing outside the museum, an American Indian person was sitting on a tree stump smoking a long peace pipe. After watching him for about five minutes, Gramps asked if he could try it.

The man passed Gramps the pipe, and Gramps

sat down on the grass, took two puffs and passed it to Gram. She didn't even blink. She took two puffs and passed it to me. There was a sweet, sticky taste on the end of the pipe. With the stem in my mouth, I gave it two little kisses, which is what it looked like Gram and Gramps had done. The smoke came into my mouth, and I held it there while I passed the pipe back.

I held that smoke in my mouth while Gram and Gramps puffed some more. I was feeling slightly whang-doodled. I opened my mouth a wee bit, and a tiny stream of smoke curled out into the air, and when I saw that, for some reason I was reminded of my mother. It didn't make any sense, but my brain was saying, "There goes your mother," and I watched the trail of smoke disappear into the air.

In the shop attached to the pipe museum, Gramps bought two peace pipes. One was for him and one was for me. "It's not for smoking with," he said. "It's for remembering with."

That night we stayed in Injun Joe's Peace Palace Motel. On a sign in the lobby, someone had crossed out "Injun" and written "Native American" so the whole sign read: "Native American Joe's Peace Palace Motel." In our room, the "Injun Joe's" embroidered on the towels had been changed with black marker to "Indian Joe's." I wished everybody would just make up their minds.

By now I was used to staying in a room with Gram and Gramps. Every night when they climbed into bed, they lay right beside each other on their backs and Gramps said, every single night, "Well, this ain't our marriage bed, but it will do."

Probably the most precious thing in the whole world to Gramps—besides Gram—was their marriage bed. This is what he called their bed back home in Bybanks, Kentucky. One of the stories that Gramps liked to tell was about how he and all his brothers had been born in that bed, and all Gram and Gramps's own children had been born in that same bed.

When Gramps tells this story, he starts with when he was seventeen years old and living with his parents in Bybanks. That's when he met Gram. She was visiting her aunt who lived over the meadow from where Gramps lived. "I was a wild thing then," Gramps said, "and I didn't stand still for any girl, I can tell you that." They had to try to catch Gramps on the run. But when he saw Gram running in the meadow, with her long hair as silky as a filly's, he was the one who was trying to do the catching. "Talk about wild things! Your grandmother was the wildest, most untamed, most ornery and beautiful creature ever to grace this earth."

Gramps said he followed her like a sick, old dog for twenty-two days, and on the twenty-third day, he marched up to her father and asked if he could marry her. Her father said, "If you can get her to stand still long enough and if she'll have you, I guess you can."

When Gramps asked Gram to marry him, she said, "Do you have a dog?" Gramps said that yes, as a matter of fact, he had a fat old beagle named Sadie. Gram said, "And where does she sleep?"

Gramps stumbled around a bit and said, "To tell you the truth, she sleeps right next to me, but if we was to get married, I—"

"And when you come in the door at night," Gram said, "what does that dog do?"

Gramps couldn't figure what she was getting at, so he just told the truth. "She jumps all over me, a-lickin' and a-howlin'."

"And then what do *you* do?" Gram said.

"Well, gosh—" Gramps said. He did not like to admit it, but he said, "I take her in my lap and pet her till she calms down, and sometimes I sing her a song. You're making me feel foolish."

"I don't mean to," she said. "You've told me all I

need to know. I figure if you treat a dog that good, you'll treat me better. I figure if that old beagle Sadie loves you so much, I'll probably love you better. Yes, I'll marry you."

They were married three months later. During that time between his proposal and their wedding day, Gramps and his father and brothers built a small house in the clearing behind the first meadow. "We didn't have time," Gramps said, "to completely finish it, and there wasn't a single stick of furniture in it yet, but that didn't matter. We were going to sleep there on our wedding night all the same."

They were married in an aspen grove on a clear July day, and afterward they and all their friends and relatives had a wedding supper on the banks of the river. During the supper, Gramps noticed that his father and two of his brothers were absent. He thought maybe they were planning a wet cheer, which is when the men kidnap the groom for an hour or so and they all go out to the woods and share a bottle of whiskey. Before the end of the supper his father and brothers came back, but they did not kidnap him for a wet cheer. Gramps was just as glad, he said, because he needed his wits about him that evening.

At the end of the supper, Gramps picked up Gram in his arms and carried her across the meadow. Behind them, everyone was singing, "Oh meet me, in the tulips, when the tulips do blooom—" This is what they always sing at weddings when the married couple leaves. It is supposed to be a joke, as if Gram and Gramps were going away by themselves and might not reappear until the following spring when the tulips were in bloom.

Gramps carried Gram all the way across the meadow and through the trees and into the clearing where their little house stood. He carried her in through the door, and took one look around and started to cry.

The reason Gramps cried when he carried Gram into the house was that there, in the center of the bedroom, stood his own parents' bed—the bed that Gramps and each of his brothers had been born in, the bed his parents had always slept in. This was where his father and brothers had disappeared to during the wedding supper. They had been moving the bed into Gram and Gramps's new house. At the foot of the bed, wiggling and slurping, was Sadie, Gramps's old beagle dog.

Gramps always ends this story by saying, "That

bed has been around my whole entire life, and I'm going to die in that bed, and then that bed will know everything there is to know about me."

So each night on our trip out to Idaho, Gramps patted the bed in the motel and said, "Well, this ain't our marriage bed, but it will do," while I lay in the next bed wondering if I would ever have a marriage bed like theirs.

13
BOUNCING BIRKWAY

IT WAS TIME TO TELL GRAM AND GRAMPS ABOUT Mr. Birkway.

Mr. Birkway was mighty strange. I didn't know what to make of him. I thought he might have a few squirrels in the attic of his brain. He was one of those energetic teachers who loved his subject half to death and leaped about the room dramatically, waving his arms and clutching his chest and whomping people on the back.

He said, "Brilliant!" and "Wonderful!" and "Terrific!" He was tall and slim, and his bushy black hair made him look wild, but he had enormous deep brown cowlike eyes that sparkled all over the place, and when he turned these eyes on you, you felt as if his whole purpose in life was to stand there and listen to you, and you alone.

Midway through the first class, Mr. Birkway asked for everyone's summer journals. He flung

himself up and down the aisles, receiving the journals as if they were manna from heaven. "Wonderful!" he said to each journal-giver.

I was worried. I had no journal.

On top of Mary Lou Finney's desk were six
journals. *Six*. Mr. Birkway said, "Heavens. Mercy.
Is it—can it be—Shakespeare?" He counted the
journals. "Six! Brilliant! Magnificent!"

Christy and Megan, two girls who had their
own club called the GGP (whatever that meant),
were whispering over on the other side of the
room and casting malevolent looks in Mary Lou's
direction. Mary Lou kept her hand on top of the
journals as Mr. Birkway reached for them. In a low
voice she said, "I don't want you to read them."

"What?" Mr. Birkway boomed. "Not *read*
them?" The whole room was silent. Mr. Birkway
scooped up Mary Lou's journals before she could
even blink. He said, "Don't be silly. Brilliant!
Thank you!"

Another girl, Beth Ann, looked as if she might
cry. Phoebe was sending me messages with her
eyebrows that indicated that she was not too
pleased either. I think they were all hoping that
Mr. Birkway was not actually going to read these
journals.

Mr. Birkway went around the whole room snatching journals. Alex Cheevey's journal was covered with basketball stickers. Christy's and Megan's were slathered over with pictures of male models. The cover of Ben's was a cartoon of a boy with a normal boy's head, but the arms and legs were pencils, and out of the tips of the hands and feet were dribbles of words.

When he got to Phoebe's desk, Mr. Birkway lifted up her plain journal and peeked inside. Phoebe was trying to slide down in her chair. "I didn't write much," Phoebe said. "In fact, I can hardly remember what I wrote about at all."

By the time Mr. Birkway got to me, my heart was clobbering around so hard I thought it might leap straight out of my chest. "Deprived child," he said. "You didn't have a chance to write a journal."

"I'm new—"

"New? How blessed," he said. "There's nothing in this whole wide world that is better than a new person!"

"So I didn't know about the journals—"

"Not to worry!" Mr. Birkway said. "I'll think of something."

I wasn't sure what that meant. I thought maybe he would give me a whole lot of extra homework or something. For the rest of the day, you could see little groups of people asking each other, "Did you write about me?" I was very glad I hadn't written anything.

For a while, we didn't hear any more about the journals. We had absolutely no idea all the trouble they were going to cause.

14
THE RHODODENDRON

ONE SATURDAY, I WAS AT PHOEBE'S AGAIN. HER FAther was golfing, and her mother was running errands. Mrs. Winterbottom had read out a long list to us of where she would be in case we needed her. If we heard any noises at all, we were supposed to call the police immediately. "After you call the police," Mrs. Winterbottom said, "call Mrs. Cadaver. I think she's home today. I'm sure she would come right over."

"Oh *sure*," Phoebe whispered to me. "That's about the last person I would call." Phoebe imagined that every noise was the lunatic sneaking in or the message-leaver creeping up to drop off another anonymous note. She was so jumpy that I began to feel uneasy too.

After her mother left, Phoebe said, "Mrs. Cadaver works odd hours, doesn't she? Sometimes she works every night for a week, straggling home when most people are waking up, but sometimes she works during the day."

"She's a nurse, so I guess she works different shifts," I said.

That day Mrs. Cadaver was home, puttering around her garden. We saw her from Phoebe's bedroom window. Actually, puttering is not the best word. What she was doing was more like slogging and slashing. Mrs. Cadaver hacked branches off of trees and hauled these to the back of her lot where she lumped them into a pile of branches that she had hacked off last week.

"I told you she was as strong as an ox," Phoebe said.

Next, Mrs. Cadaver slashed and sliced at a pitiful rosebush that had been trying to creep up the side of her house. Then she sheared off the tops of the hedge that borders Phoebe's yard. She moved on to a rhododendron bush, which she was poking and prodding when a car pulled into her driveway. A tall man with bushy black hair leaped out and, seeing her, he practically skipped back to where she was. They hugged each other.

"Oh no," Phoebe said. The man with the bushy black hair was Mr. Birkway, our English teacher.

Mrs. Cadaver pointed to the rhododendron

bush and then at the axe, but Mr. Birkway shook his head. He disappeared into the garage and returned with two shovels. Then he and Mrs. Cadaver gouged and prodded and tunneled around in the dirt until the poor old rhododendron flopped onto its side. They lugged the bush to the opposite side of the yard where there was a mound of dirt, and they replanted the bush.

"Maybe there's something hidden under the bush," Phoebe said.

"Like what?"

"Like Mr. Cadaver—as I told you before. Maybe Mr. Birkway helped her chop up her husband and bury him and maybe they were getting worried and decided to disguise the spot with a rhododendron bush." I must have looked skeptical. Phoebe said, "Sal, you never can tell. And Sal, I don't think you or your father should go over there anymore."

I certainly agreed with her on that one. Dad and I had been there two nights earlier, and I had hardly been able to sit still. I started noticing all these frightening things in Margaret's house: creepy masks, old swords, books with titles like *The Murders in the Rue Morgue* and *The Skull and the Hatchet*. Margaret cornered me in the kitchen and said, "So what has your father told you about me?"

"Nothing," I said.

"Oh." She seemed disappointed.

My father's behavior was always different at Margaret's. At home, I would sometimes find him sitting on his bed staring at the floor, or reading through old letters, or gazing at the photo album. He looked sad and lonely. But at Margaret's, he would smile, and sometimes even laugh, and once she touched his hand, and he let her hand rest there on top of his. I didn't like it. I didn't want my father to be sad, but at least when he was sad, I knew he was remembering my mother. So when Phoebe suggested that my father and I should not go to Margaret's, I was quite willing to agree with that notion.

When Phoebe's mother came home from running all her errands, she looked terrible. She was sniffling and blowing her nose.

Phoebe said that we were going to do our homework. Upstairs, I said, "Maybe we should have helped her put away the groceries."

"She likes to do all that by herself," Phoebe said.

"Are you sure?"

"Of course I'm sure," Phoebe said. "I've lived here my whole life, haven't I?"

"She looked as if she'd been crying. Maybe something is wrong. Maybe something is bothering her."

"Don't you think she would say so then?"

"Maybe she's afraid to," I said. I wondered why it was so easy for me to see that Phoebe's mother was worried and miserable, but Phoebe couldn't see it—or if she could, she was ignoring it. Maybe she didn't *want* to notice. Maybe it was too frightening a thing. I wondered if this was how it had been with my mother. Were there things I didn't notice?

Later that afternoon, when Phoebe and I went downstairs, Mrs. Winterbottom was talking with Prudence. "Do you think I lead a tiny life?" she asked.

"How do you mean?" Prudence said, as she filed her nails. "Do we have any nail polish remover?"

Phoebe's mother retrieved a bottle of nail polish remover from the bathroom.

"Oh!" Prudence said. "Before I forget—do you think you could sew up the hem on my brown skirt so I could wear it tomorrow? Oh, please?"

Prudence tilted her head to the side, tugged at her hair in exactly the same way Phoebe does, and smooshed up her mouth into a little pout.

"Doesn't Prudence know how to sew?" I asked.

"Of course she does," Phoebe said. "Why?"

"I was just wondering why she doesn't sew her own skirt."

"Sal, you're becoming very critical."

Before I left Phoebe's that day, Mrs. Winterbottom handed Prudence her brown skirt with the newly sewn hem, and all the way home I wondered about Mrs. Winterbottom and what she meant about living a tiny life. If she didn't like all that baking and cleaning and jumping up to get bottles of nail polish remover and sewing hems, why did she do it? Why didn't she tell them to do some of these things themselves? Maybe she was afraid there would be nothing left for her to do. There would be no need for her and she would become invisible and no one would notice.

When I got home that day, my father handed me a package. "It's from Margaret," he said.

"What is it?"

"I don't know. Why don't you open it?"

Inside was a blue sweater. I put it back in the box and went upstairs. My father followed me.

"Sal—? Sal—do you like it?"

"I don't want it," I said.

"She was just trying to—she likes you—"

"I don't care if she likes me or not," I said.

My father stood there looking around the room. "I want to tell you something about Margaret," he said.

"Well, I don't want to hear it." I was feeling so completely ornery. When my father left the room, I could still hear my own voice saying, "I don't want to hear it." I sounded exactly like Phoebe.

15
A SNAKE HAS A SNACK

It was hotter than blazes in South Dakota. In Sioux Falls, Gramps took off his shirt. Passing Mitchell, Gram unbuttoned her dress down to her waist. Just beyond Chamberlain, Gramps took a detour to the Missouri River. He parked the car beneath a tree overlooking a sandy bank.

Gram and Gramps kicked off their shoes. It was quiet and hot, hot, hot. All you could hear was a crow calling somewhere up river and the distant sound of cars along the highway. The hot air pressed against my face, and my hair was like a hot, heavy blanket draped on my neck and back. It was so hot you could smell the heat baking the stones and dirt along the bank.

Gram pulled her dress up over her head, and Gramps undid his buckle and let his pants slide to the ground. They started kicking water at each other and scooping it up and letting it run down their faces. They walked in to where it was knee deep and sat down.

"Come on, chickabiddy," Gramps called.

Gram said, "It's delicious!"

I gazed up and down the river. Not a soul in sight. The water looked cool and clear. Gram and Gramps sat there in the river, grinning away. I waded in and sat down. It was nearly heaven, with that cool water rippling and a high, clear sky all around us, and trees waving along the banks.

My hair floated all around me. My mother's hair had been long and black, like mine, but a week before she left, she cut it. My father said to me, "Don't cut yours, Sal. Please don't cut yours."

My mother said, "I knew you wouldn't like it if I cut mine."

My father said, "I didn't say anything about yours."

"But I know what you're thinking," she said.

"I loved your hair, Sugar," he said.

I saved her hair. I swept it up from the kitchen floor and wrapped it in a plastic bag and hid it beneath the floorboards of my room. It was still there, along with the postcards she sent.

As Gram, Gramps, and I sat in the Missouri River, I tried not to think of the postcards. I tried to concentrate on the high sky and the cool water. It would have been perfect except for that ornery crow calling away: *car-car-car.* "Will we be here long?" I asked.

The boy came out of nowhere. Gramps saw him first and whispered, "Get behind me, chickabiddy. You too," he said to Gram. The boy was about fifteen or sixteen, with shaggy dark hair. He wore blue jeans and no shirt, and his chest was brown and muscular. In his hand he held a long bowie knife, its sheath fastened to his belt. He stood next to Gramps's pants on the bank.

I thought of Phoebe and knew that if she were here, she would be warning us that the boy was a lunatic who would hack us all to pieces. I was wishing we had never stopped at the river, and that my grandparents would be more cautious, maybe even a little more like Phoebe, who saw danger everywhere.

As the boy stared at us, Gramps said, "Howdy."

The boy said, "This here's private property."

Gramps looked all around. "Is it? I didn't see any signs."

"It's private property."

"Why heck," Gramps said, "this here's a river. I never heard of no river being private property."

The boy picked up Gramps's pants and slid his hand into a pocket. "This land where I'm standing is private property."

I was frightened of the boy and wanted Gramps to do something, but Gramps looked cool and calm. He sounded as if he hadn't a care in the world, but I knew that he was worried by the way he kept inching in front of me and Gram.

I felt around the riverbed, pulled up a flat stone, and skimmed it across the water. The boy watched the stone, counting the skips.

A snake flickered along the bank and slid into the water.

"See that tree?" Gramps said. He pointed to an old willow leaning into the water near where the boy stood.

"I see it," the boy said, sliding his hand into another of Gramps's pockets.

Gramps said, "See that knothole? Watch what this here chickabiddy can do to a knothole." Gramps winked at me. The veins in his neck were standing out. You could practically see the blood rushing through them.

I felt around the riverbed and pulled up another flat, jagged rock. I had done this a million times in the swimming hole in Bybanks. I pulled my arm back and tossed the rock straight at the tree. One edge embedded itself in the knothole. The boy stopped rummaging through Gramps's pockets and eyed me.

Gram said, "Oh!" and flailed at the water. She reached down, pulled up a snake, and gave Gramps a puzzled look. "It's a water moccasin, isn't it?" she said. "It's a poisonous one, isn't it?" The snake slithered and wriggled, straining toward the water. "I do believe it has had a snack out of my leg." She stared hard at Gramps.

The boy stood on the bank holding Gramps's wallet. Gramps scooped up Gram and carried her out of the water. "Would you mind dropping that thing?" he said to Gram, who was still clutching the snake. To me he said, "Get on out of there, chickabiddy."

As Gramps put Gram on the riverbank, the boy came and knelt beside her. "I'm sure glad you have that knife," Gramps said, reaching for it. As he made a slit in Gram's leg across the snake bite, blood trickled down her ankle. I grabbed Gram's hand as she stared up at the sky. Gramps knelt to suck out the wound, but the boy said, "Here, I'll do it." The boy placed his mouth against Gram's bloody leg. He sucked and spit, sucked and spit.

Gram's eyelids fluttered.

"Can you point us to a hospital?" Gramps said.

The boy nodded as he spit. Gramps and the boy carried Gram to the car and settled her in the back seat while I snatched their clothes from the riverbank. We placed Gram's head on my lap and her feet on the boy's lap, and all the while the boy continued sucking and spitting. In between, he gave directions to the hospital. Gram held onto my hand.

Gramps, still in his boxer shorts, and dripping wet, carried Gram into the hospital. The boy's mouth hovered over her leg the whole time, sucking and spitting.

Gram spent the night in the hospital. In the waiting room, the boy from the riverbank sprawled in a chair. I offered him a paper towel. "You've got blood on your mouth," I said. I handed him a fifty-dollar bill. "My grandfather said to give you this. That's all the cash he has right now. He said to tell you thanks. He'd come out himself, but he doesn't want to leave her."

He looked at the fifty-dollar bill in my hand. "I don't need it."

"You don't have to stay," I said.

He glanced around the waiting room. "I know

it." He looked away and then said, "I like your hair."

"I was thinking of cutting it."

"Don't."

I sat down beside him.

He said, "It wasn't really private property."

"I didn't think so."

Later, when I went in to see Gram, she was all tucked up in bed, pale and sleepy. Next to her on the narrow bed, Gramps was lying on top of the covers, stroking her hair. A nurse came in and made him get off the bed. He had, by now, put his pants on, but he looked a wreck.

I asked Gram how she was feeling. She blinked her eyes a few times and said, "Piddles."

Gramps said, "They must've given her something. She doesn't know what she's saying."

I leaned down and whispered in her ear. "Gram, don't leave us."

"Piddles," Gram said.

When the nurse left the room, Gramps climbed back on top of the bed and lay down next to Gram. He patted the bed. "Well," he said, "this ain't our marriage bed, but it will do."

16
THE SINGING TREE

GRAM WAS RELEASED FROM THE HOSPITAL THE NEXT morning mainly because she was so ornery. Gramps wanted her to stay another day, but Gram climbed out of bed and said, "Where's my underwear?"

"I guess this cantankerous woman is getting out of here," Gramps said.

I think fear had made us all a little cantankerous. I had spent the night in the waiting room. Gramps offered to get me a motel room, but I was afraid that if I left the hospital, I would never see Gram again. The boy we had met at the river curled up in an armchair, but I don't think he slept either. Once he used the telephone. I heard him say, "Yeah, I'll be home in the morning. I'm with some friends."

The boy woke me up at six o'clock and said Gram was much better. He handed me a piece of paper. "It's my address, in case you ever want to write or anything, but I'd understand if you didn't—"

I opened the paper. "What's your name?"

He smiled. "Oh yeah, right." He took the paper and added his name: Tom Fleet. "See ya," he said.

As we were checking out of the hospital, I asked if we should call my father. Gramps said, "Well, now, chickabiddy, I thought about that, but it's only going to make him worry. Do you think we could wait to call him when we get to Idaho?"

Gramps was right, but I was disappointed. I was ready to call my father. I wanted very much to hear his voice, but I was also afraid that I might ask him to come and get me.

Outside the hospital, I heard the warbling of a bird, and it was such a familiar warble that I stopped and listened for its source. Bordering the parking lot was a rim of poplars. The sound was coming from somewhere in the top of one of those trees, and I thought, instantly, of the singing tree in Bybanks.

Next to my favorite sugar maple tree beside the barn is a tall aspen. When I was younger, I heard the most beautiful birdsong coming from the top of that tree. It was not a call; it was a true birdsong, with trills and warbles. I stood beneath that tree for the longest time, hoping to catch sight of the bird who was singing such a song. I saw no bird— only leaves waving in the breeze. The longer I stared up at the leaves, the more it seemed that it was the tree itself that was singing. Every time I passed that tree, I listened. Sometimes it sang, sometimes it did not, but from then on I always called it the singing tree.

The morning after my father learned that my mother was not coming back, he left for Lewiston, Idaho. Gram and Gramps came to stay with me. I had pleaded to go along, but my father said he didn't think I should have to go through that. That day I climbed up into the maple and watched the singing tree, waiting for it to sing. I stayed there all day and on into the early evening. It did not sing.

At dusk, Gramps placed three sleeping bags at the foot of the tree, and he, Gram, and I slept there all night. The tree did not sing.

In the hospital parking lot, Gram heard the song, too. "Oh Salamanca," she said. "A singing tree!" She pulled at Gramps's sleeve.

"Oh, it's a good sign, don't you think?"

As we swept on across South Dakota toward

the Badlands, the whispers no longer said, *hurry, hurry* or *rush, rush*. They now said, *slow down, slow down*. I could not figure this out. It seemed some sort of warning, but I did not have too much time to think about it, as I was busy telling about Phoebe.

17
In the Course of a Lifetime

A FEW DAYS AFTER PHOEBE AND I HAD SEEN MR. Birkway and Mrs. Cadaver whacking away at the rhododendron, I walked home with Phoebe after school. She was as crotchety and sullen as a three-legged mule, and I was not quite sure why. She had been asking me why I had not said anything to my father about Mrs. Cadaver and Mr. Birkway, and I told her that I was waiting for the right time.

"Your father was over there yesterday," Phoebe said. "I saw him. He'd better watch out. What would you do if Mrs. Cadaver chopped up your father? Would you go live with your mother?"

It surprised me when she said that, reminding me that I had told Phoebe nothing about my mother. "Yes, I suppose I would go live with her." That was impossible and I knew it, but for some reason I could not tell Phoebe that, so I lied.

Phoebe's mother was sitting at the kitchen table

when we walked in. In front of her was a pan of burned brownies. She blew her nose. "Oh sweetie," she said, "you startled me. How was it?"

"How was what?" Phoebe said.

"Why, sweetie, school of course. How was it? How were your classes?"

"Okay."

"Just okay?" Mrs. Winterbottom suddenly leaned over and kissed Phoebe's cheek.

"I'm not a baby, you know," Phoebe said, wiping off the kiss.

Mrs. Winterbottom stabbed the brownies with a knife. "Want one?" she asked.

"They're burned," Phoebe said. "Besides, I'm too fat."

"Oh sweetie, you're not fat," Mrs. Winterbottom said.

"I am."

"No, you're not."

"I am, I am, I am!" Phoebe shouted at her mother. "You don't have to bake things for me. I'm too fat. And you don't have to wait here for me to come home. I'm thirteen now."

Phoebe marched upstairs. Mrs. Winterbottom offered me a brownie, so I sat down at the table. What I started doing was remembering the day before my mother left. I did not know it was to be her last day home. Several times that day, my mother asked me if I wanted to walk up in the fields with her. It was drizzling outside, and I was cleaning out my desk, and I just did not feel like going. "Maybe later," I kept saying. When she asked me for about the tenth time, I said, "No! I don't want to go. Why do you keep asking me?" I don't know why I did that. I didn't mean anything by it, but that was one of the last memories she had of me, and I wished I could take it back.

Phoebe's sister, Prudence, stormed into the house, slamming the door behind her. "I blew it, I just know it!" she wailed.

"Oh sweetie," her mother said.

"I did!" Prudence said. "I did, I did, I did."

Mrs. Winterbottom half-heartedly chipped away at the burned brownies and asked Prudence if she would have another chance at cheerleading tryouts.

"Yes, tomorrow. But I know I'm going to blow it!"

Her mother said, "Maybe I'll come along and watch." I could tell that Mrs. Winterbottom was trying to rise above some awful sadness she was feeling, but Prudence couldn't see that. Prudence had her own agenda, just as I had had my own agenda that day my mother wanted me to walk with her. I couldn't see my own mother's sadness.

"What?" Prudence said. "Come along and *watch*?"

"Yes, wouldn't that be nice?"

"No!" Prudence said. "No, no, no. You can't. It would be awful."

I heard the front door open and shut and Phoebe came in the kitchen waving a white envelope. "Guess what was on the steps?" she said.

Mrs. Winterbottom took the envelope and turned it over and over before she slowly unsealed it and slipped out the message.

"Oh," she said. "Who is doing this?" She held out the piece of paper: *In the course of a lifetime, what does it matter?*

Prudence said, "Well, I have more important things to worry about, I can assure you. I know I'm going to blow those cheerleading tryouts. I just know it."

On and on she went, until Phoebe said, "Cripes, Prudence, in the course of a lifetime, what does it matter?"

At that moment, it was as if a switch went off in Mrs. Winterbottom's brain. She put her hand to her mouth and stared out the window. She was invisible to Prudence and Phoebe, though. They did not notice.

Phoebe said, "Are these cheerleading tryouts such a big deal? Will you even remember them in five years?"

"Yes!" Prudence said. "Yes, I most certainly will."

"How about ten years? Will you remember them in ten?"

"Yes!" Prudence said.

As I walked home, I thought about the message. *In the course of a lifetime, what does it matter?* I said it over and over. I wondered about the mysterious messenger, and I wondered about all the things in the course of a lifetime that would not matter. I did not think cheerleading tryouts would matter, but I was not so sure about yelling at your mother. I was certain, however, that if your mother left, it would be something that mattered in the whole long course of your lifetime.

18
THE GOOD MAN

I SHOULD MENTION MY FATHER.

When I was telling Phoebe's story to Gram and Gramps, I did not say much about my father. He was their son, and not only did they know him better than I, but as Gram often said, he was the light of their lives. They had three other sons at one time, but one son died when a tractor flipped over on him, one was killed when he skied into a tree, and the third died when he jumped into the freezing cold Ohio River to save his best friend (the best friend survived but my uncle did not).

My father was the only son left, but even if their other sons were still alive, my father might still be their light because he is also a kind, honest, simple, and good man. I do not mean simple as in simple-minded—I mean he likes plain and simple things. His favorite clothes are the flannel shirts and blue jeans that he has had for twenty years. It nearly killed him to buy white shirts and a suit for his new job in Euclid.

He loved the farm because he could be out in the real air, and he wouldn't wear work gloves because he liked to touch the earth and the wood and the animals. It was painful for him to go to work in an office when we moved. He did not like being sealed up inside with nothing real to touch.

We'd had the same car, a blue Chevy, for fifteen years. He couldn't bear to part with it because he had touched—and repaired—every inch of it. I also think he couldn't bear the thought that if he sold it, someone might take it to the junkyard. My father hated the whole idea of putting cars out to pasture. He often prowled through junkyards touching old cars and buying old alternators and carburetors just for the joy of cleaning them up and making them work again. My grandfather had never quite gotten the hang of car mechanics, and so he thought my father was a genius.

My mother was right when she said my father was good. He was always thinking of little things to cheer up someone else. This nearly drove my mother crazy because I think she wanted to keep up with him, but it was not her natural gift like it was with my father. He would be out in the field and see a flowering bush that my grandmother might like, and he would dig the whole thing up and take it straight over to Gram's garden and re-plant it. If it snowed, he would be up at dawn to trek over to his parents' house and shovel out their driveway.

If he went into town to buy supplies for the farm, he would come back with something for my mother and something for me. They were small things—a cotton scarf, a book, a glass paper-weight—but whatever he brought, it was exactly what you would have picked out for yourself.

I had never seen him angry. "Sometimes I don't think you're human," my mother told him. It was the sort of thing she said just before she left, and it bothered me, because it seemed as if she wanted him to be meaner, less good.

Two days before she left, when I first heard her raise the subject of leaving, she said, "I feel so rotten in comparison."

"Sugar, you're not rotten," he said.

"See?" she said. "See? Why couldn't you at least believe I am rotten?"

"Because you're not," he said.

She said she had to leave in order to clear her head, and to clear her heart of all the bad things.

She needed to learn about what she was.

"You can do that here, Sugar," he said.

"I need to do it on my own," she said. "I can't think. All I see here is what I am not. I am not brave. I am not good. And I wish someone would call me by my real name. My name isn't Sugar. It's Chanhassen."

She had not been well. She had had some terrible shocks, it is true, but I did not understand why she could not get better with us. I begged her to take me with her, but she said I could not miss school and my father needed me and besides, she had to go alone. She *had* to.

I thought she might change her mind, or at least tell me when she was leaving. But she did neither of those things. She left me a letter which explained that if she said good-bye, it would be too terribly painful and it would sound too permanent. She wanted me to know that she would think of me every minute and that she would be back before the tulips bloomed.

But, of course, she was not back before the tulips bloomed.

It nearly killed my father after she left, I know it, but he continued on doing everything just as before, whistling and humming and finding little gifts for people. He kept bringing home gifts for my mother and stacking them in a pile in their bedroom.

On the day after he found out she wasn't returning, he flew to Lewiston, Idaho, and when he came back, he spent three days chipping away at the fireplace hidden behind the plaster wall. Some of the cement grouting between the bricks had to be replaced, and he wrote her name in the new cement. He wrote *Chanhassen*, not *Sugar*.

Three weeks later he put the farm up for sale. By this time he was receiving letters from Mrs. Cadaver, and I knew that he was answering her letters. Then he drove up to see Mrs. Cadaver while I stayed with Gram and Gramps. When he came back, he said we were moving to Euclid. Mrs. Cadaver had helped him find a job.

I didn't even wonder how he had met Mrs. Cadaver or how long he had known her. I ignored her whole existence. Besides, I was too busy throwing the most colossal temper tantrums. I refused to move. I would not leave our farm, our maple tree, our swimming hole, our pigs, our chickens, our hayloft. I would not leave the place that belonged to me. I would not leave the place to which, I was convinced, my mother might return.

At first my father did not argue with me. He let me behave like a wild boar. At last, he took down the For Sale sign and put up a For Rent sign. He said he would rent out the farm, hire someone to care for the animals and the crops, and rent a house for us in Euclid. The farm would still belong to us and one day we could return to it. "But for now," he said, "we have to leave because your mother is haunting me day and night. She's in the fields, the air, the barn, the walls, the trees." He said we were making this move to learn about bravery and courage. That sounded awfully familiar.

In the end, I think I merely ran out of steam. I stopped throwing tantrums. I didn't help pack, but when the time came, I climbed in the car and joined my father for our move to Euclid. I did not feel brave, and I did not feel courageous.

When I told my story of Phoebe to Gram and Gramps, I mentioned none of this. They knew it already. They knew my father was a good man, they knew I did not want to leave the farm, they knew my father felt we had to leave. They also knew that my father had tried, many times, to explain to me about Margaret, but that I wouldn't hear it.

On that long day that my father and I left the

farm behind and drove to Euclid, I wished that my father was not such a good man, so there would be someone to blame for my mother's leaving. I didn't want to blame her. She was my mother, and she was part of me.

19
FISH IN THE AIR

GRAM SAID, "WHERE DID WE LEAVE OFF WITH Peeby? What was happening?"

"What's the matter, gooseberry?" Gramps said. "Did that snake bite your brains?"

"No," she said. "It did not bite my brains. I was just trying to refresh my memory."

"Let's see," Gramps said, "didn't Peeby want you to tell your daddy about Mrs. Cadaver and Mr. Birkway hacking up her husband?"

Yes, that is what Phoebe wanted, and it is what I tried to do. One Sunday, when my father was looking through the photo albums, I asked him if he knew much about Mrs. Cadaver. He looked up quickly. "You're ready to talk about Margaret?" he said.

"Well—there were a few things I wanted to mention—"

"I've been wanting to explain—" he said.

I plunged on. I didn't want him to explain. I wanted to warn him. "Phoebe and I saw her slashing and hacking away at the bushes in her backyard."

"Is there something wrong with that?" he asked.

I tried another approach. "Her voice is like dead leaves blowing around, and her hair is spooky."

"I see," he said.

"And there is a man who visits her—"

"Sal, that sounds like spying."

"And I don't think we should go over there anymore."

Dad took off his glasses and rubbed them on his shirt for about five minutes. Then he said, "Sal, you're trying to catch fish in the air. Your mother is not coming back."

It looked like I was merely jealous of Mrs. Cadaver. There in the calm light of my father, all those things that Phoebe had said about Mrs. Cadaver seemed foolish.

"I'd like to explain about her," my father said.

"Oh, never mind. Just forget I mentioned her. I don't need any explanations."

Later, when I was doing my homework, I found myself doodling in the margin of my English book. I had drawn a figure of a woman with wild hair and evil eyes and a rope around her neck. I drew a tree, fastened the rope to it, and hung her.

The next day at school, I studied Mr. Birkway as he leaped and cavorted about the classroom. If he was a murderer, he certainly was a lively one. I had always pictured murderers as being mopey and sullen. I hoped Mr. Birkway was in love with Margaret Cadaver and would marry her and take her away so that my father and I could go back to Bybanks.

What I found most surprising about Mr. Birkway was that he increasingly reminded me of my mother—or at least of my mother *before* the sadness set in. There was a liveliness to both Mr. Birkway and my mother, and an excitement—a passion—for words and for stories.

That day, as Mr. Birkway talked about Greek mythology, I started daydreaming about my mother, who loved books almost as much as she loved all her outdoor treasures. She liked to carry little books in her pocket and sometimes when we were out in the fields, she would flop down in the grass and start reading aloud.

My mother especially liked Indian stories. She knew about thunder gods, earth-makers, wise crows, sly coyotes, and shadow souls. Her favorite stories were those about people who came back, after death, as a bird or a river or a horse. She even knew one story about an old warrior who came back as a potato.

The next thing I knew, Mr. Birkway was saying, "Right, Phoebe? Are you awake? You have the second report."

"Report?" Phoebe said.

Mr. Birkway clutched his heart. "Ben is doing an oral report on Prometheus this Friday. You're doing one on Pandora next Monday."

"Lucky me," Phoebe muttered.

Mr. Birkway asked me to stay after class for a minute. Phoebe sent me warning messages with her eyebrows. As everyone else was leaving the room, Phoebe said, "I'll stay with you if you want."

"Why?"

"Because of him hacking up Mr. Cadaver, that's what. I don't think you should be alone with him."

He did not hack me up. Instead, he gave me a special assignment, a "mini journal." "I don't know what that is," I said. Phoebe was breathing on my shoulder. Mr. Birkway said I should write about something that interested me. "Like what?" I said.

"Oh, a place, a room, a person—don't worry about it too much. Just write whatever comes to mind."

Phoebe and I walked home with Mary Lou and Ben. My brain was a mess, what with trying not to flinch whenever Ben brushed against me. When we left Ben and Mary Lou and turned the corner onto Phoebe's street, I wasn't paying much attention. I suppose I was aware that someone was coming along the sidewalk in our direction, but it wasn't until the person was about three feet away that I really took notice.

It was Phoebe's lunatic, coming toward us, staring right at us. He stopped directly in front of us, blocking our way.

"Phoebe Winterbottom, right?" he said to Phoebe.

Her voice was a little squeak. The only sound that came out was a tiny "Erp—"

"What's the matter?" he said. He slid one hand into his pocket.

Phoebe pushed him, yanked my arm, and started running. "Oh-my-god!" she said. "Oh-my-god!"

I was grateful that we were nearly at Phoebe's

house, so if he stabbed us in broad daylight, maybe one of her neighbors would discover our bodies and take us to the hospital before we bled entirely to death. I was beginning to believe he was a lunatic.

Phoebe tugged at her doorknob, but the door was locked. Phoebe beat on the door, and her mother suddenly pulled it open. She looked rather pale and shaken herself.

"It was locked!" Phoebe said. "Why was the door locked?"

"Oh sweetie," Mrs. Winterbottom said. "It's just that—I thought that—" She peered around us and looked up and down the street. "Did you see someone—did someone frighten you—"

"It was the lunatic," Phoebe said. "We saw him just now." She could hardly catch her breath. "Maybe we should call the police—or tell Dad."

I took a good long look at Phoebe's mother. She did not seem capable of phoning the police or Mr. Winterbottom. I think she was more scared than we were. She went around locking all the doors.

Nothing more happened that evening, and by the time I went home, the lunatic did not seem quite so threatening. No one called the police, and to my knowledge, Mrs. Winterbottom had not yet told Mr. Winterbottom, but right before I left Phoebe's house, Phoebe said to me, "If I see the lunatic once more, I'll phone the police myself."

20
THE BLACKBERRY KISS

THAT NIGHT I TRIED TO WRITE THE MINI JOURNAL
for Mr. Birkway. First I made a list of all the things
I liked, and they were all things from Bybanks—
the trees, the cows, the chickens, the pigs, the
fields, the swimming hole. It was a complete jum-
ble of things, and when I tried to write about any
one of those things, I ended up writing about my
mother, because everything was connected to her.
At last, I wrote about the blackberry kiss.

One morning when I awoke very early, I saw
my mother walking up the hill to the barn. Mist
hung about the ground, finches were singing in the
oak tree beside the house, and there was my
mother, her pregnant belly sticking out in front of
her. She was strolling up the hill, swinging her
arms and singing:

Oh, don't fall in love with a sailor boy,

A sailor boy, a sailor boy—
Oh, don't fall in love with a sailor boy,
'Cause he'll take your heart to sea—

As she approached the corner of the barn where the sugar maple stands, she plucked a few blackberries from a stray bush and popped them into her mouth. She looked all around her—back at the house, across the fields, and up into the canopy of branches overhead. She took several quick steps up to the trunk of the maple, threw her arms around it, and kissed that tree soundly.

Later that day, I examined this tree trunk. I tried to wrap my arms about it, but the trunk was much bigger than it had seemed from my window. I looked up at where her mouth must have touched the trunk. I probably imagined this, but I thought I could detect a small dark stain, as from a blackberry kiss.

I put my ear against the trunk and listened. I faced that tree squarely and kissed it firmly. To this day, I can smell the smell of the bark—a sweet, woody smell—and feel the ridges in the bark, and taste that distinctive taste on my lips.

In my mini journal, I confessed that I had since kissed all different kinds of trees, and each family of trees—oaks, maples, elms, birches—had a special flavor all its own. Mixed in with each tree's own taste was the slight taste of blackberries, and why this was so, I could not explain.

The next day, I turned in this story to Mr. Birkway. He didn't read it or even look at it, but he said, "Marvelous! Brilliant!" as he slipped it into his briefcase. "I'll put it with the other journals."

Phoebe said, "Did you write about me?"

Ben said, "Did you write about me?"

Mr. Birkway bounded around the room as if the opportunity to teach us was his notion of paradise. He read a poem by e. e. cummings titled "the little horse is newlY" and the reason why the only capital letter in the title is the Y at the end of *newlY* is because Mr. Cummings liked to do it that way.

"He probably never took English," Phoebe said.

To me that Y looked like the newly born horse standing up on his thin legs.

The poem was about a newlY born horse who doesn't know anything but feels everything. He lives in a "smoothbeautifully folded" world. I liked that. I was not sure what it was, but I liked it. Everything sounded soft and safe.

That day, Phoebe left school early for a dentist

appointment. I started walking home alone, but Ben joined me. I was completely unprepared for what happened on the way home, and for what would happen later. Ben and I were simply walking along and he said, "Did anyone ever read your palm?"

"No."

"I know how to do it," he said. "Want me to read yours?" He took my hand and stared at it for the longest time. His own hand was soft and warm. Mine was sweating like crazy. He was saying, "Hm" and tracing the lines of my palm with his finger. It gave me the shivers, but not in an entirely unpleasant way. The sun was beating down on us, and I thought it might be nice to stay there forever with him just running his finger along my palm like that. I thought about the newlY born horse who knows nothing and feels everything. I thought about the smoothbeautifully folded world. Finally, Ben said, "Do you want the good news first or the bad news?"

"The bad news. It isn't real bad, is it?"

He coughed. "The bad news is that I can't really read palms." (I snatched my hand away.) "Don't you want to know the good news?" he asked. (I started walking.) "The good news is that you let me hold your hand for almost five minutes and you didn't flinch once."

I didn't know what to make of him. He walked me all the way to my house, even though I refused to speak to him. He waited on the porch until I was ready to go to Phoebe's, and then he walked me to her house.

When I knocked at Phoebe's door, Ben said, "I'll be going now." I took a quick look at him and turned back to the door, but in that instant that I was turning my head, he leaned forward, and I do believe his lips kissed my ear. I was not sure this was what he intended. In fact, I was not sure it happened at all, because before I knew it, he had hopped down the steps and was walking away.

The door inched open and there was Phoebe's round face, as white and frightened as ever you could imagine. "Quick," she said. "Come in." She led me into the kitchen. On the kitchen table was an apple pie, and beside it were three envelopes: one for Phoebe, one for Prudence, and one for their father.

"I opened my note," Phoebe said, showing it to me. It said, *Keep all the doors locked and call your father if you need anything. I love you, Phoebe.* It was signed, *Mom.*

I didn't think too much of it. "Phoebe—" I said.

"I know, I know. It doesn't sound terrible or anything. In fact, my first thought was, 'Well, good. She knows I am old enough to be here by myself.' I figured she was out shopping or maybe she even decided to return to work, even though she wasn't supposed to go back to Rocky's Rubber until next week. But then Prudence came home and opened her note."

Phoebe showed me the note left for Prudence. It said, *Please heat up the spaghetti sauce and boil the spaghetti. I love you, Prudence.* It was signed, *Mom.*

I still didn't think too much of it, but Phoebe was suspicious. Prudence made the spaghetti, while I helped Phoebe set the table. Phoebe and I even made a salad. "I do feel sort of independent," Phoebe said.

When Phoebe's father came home, Phoebe showed him his note. He opened it and sat down, staring at the piece of paper. Phoebe looked over his shoulder and read his note aloud: *I had to go away. I can't explain. I'll call you in a few days.*

I had a sinking, sinking feeling.

Prudence started asking a million questions. "What does she mean? Go away where? Why can't she explain? Why didn't she tell you? Did she mention this? A few *days*? Where did she go?"

"Maybe we should call the police," Phoebe said. "I think she was kidnapped or something."

"Oh, Phoebe," Mr. Winterbottom said.

"I'm serious," she said. "Maybe a lunatic came in the house and dragged her off—"

"Phoebe, that is not funny."

"I'm not being funny. I mean it. It could happen."

Prudence was still asking her questions. "Where did she go? Why didn't she mention this? Didn't she tell you? Where did she go?"

"Prudence, I honestly cannot say," her father said.

"I think we should call the police," Phoebe repeated.

"Phoebe, if she was kidnapped, would the lunatic—as you say—allow her to sit down and write these notes? Mm?"

He stood up, removed his coat, and said, "Let's eat."

As I left, Phoebe said, "My mother has disappeared. Sal, don't tell anyone. Don't tell a soul."

At home, my father was slumped over the photo album. He used to close the album quickly when I came in the room, as if he were embarrassed to be caught with it. Lately, however, he didn't bother to close it. It was as if he didn't have the strength to do that.

On the opened page was a photo of my father and mother sitting in the grass beneath the sugar maple. His arms were around her and she was sort of folded into him. His face was pressed up next to hers and their hair blended together. They looked like they were connected.

"Phoebe's mother went away," I said.

He looked up at me.

"She left some notes. She says she's coming back, but I don't believe it."

I went upstairs and tried to work on my mythology report. My father came to the doorway and said, "People usually come back."

Now I can see that he was just talking in general, just trying to be comforting, but then—that night—what I heard in what he said was the tiniest reassurance of something I had been thinking and hoping. I had been praying that a miracle would happen and my mother would come back and we would return to Bybanks and everything would be exactly as it used to be.

21
SOULS

AT SCHOOL THE NEXT DAY, PHOEBE WORE A FIXED expression: a sealed, thin smile. It must have been hard for her to maintain that smile, because by the time English class came around, her chin was quivering from the strain. She was extremely quiet all day. She didn't speak to anyone but me, and the only thing she said to me was, "Stay at my house tomorrow night." It wasn't a question; it was a command.

Mr. Birkway gave us a fifteen-second exercise. As fast as we could, without thinking, we were to draw something. He would tell us what we were to draw when everyone was ready. "Remember," he said. *"Don't think.* Just draw. Fifteen seconds. Ready? Draw your *soul*. Go."

We all wasted five seconds staring blankly back at him. When we saw that he was serious and was watching the clock, our pencils hit the paper. I wasn't thinking. There wasn't time to think.

When Mr. Birkway called "Stop!" everyone looked up, dazed. Then we looked down at our papers, and a buzz went around the room. We were surprised at what had come out of our pencils.

Mr. Birkway zipped around, scooping up the papers. He shuffled them and tacked them up on the bulletin board. He said, "We now have everyone's soul captured." We all crowded around.

The first thing I noticed was that every single person had drawn a central shape—a heart, circle, square, or triangle. I thought that was unusual. I mean, no one drew a bus or a spaceship or a cow—they all drew these same shapes. Next, I noticed that inside each figure was a distinct design. At first it seemed that every one was different. There was a cross, a dark scribble, an eye, a mouth, a window.

There was one with a teardrop inside that I thought must be Phoebe's.

Then Mary Lou said, "Look at that—two are exactly the same." People were saying, "Geez" and "Wow" and "Whose are those?"

The duplicate designs were: a circle with a large maple leaf in the center, the tips of the leaf touching the sides of the circle. One of the maple leaf circles was mine. The other was Ben's.

22
EVIDENCE

I SPENT THE NEXT NIGHT AT PHOEBE'S HOUSE, BUT I could hardly sleep. Phoebe kept saying, "Hear that noise?" and she would jump up to peer out the window in case it was the lunatic returning for the rest of us. Once she saw Mrs. Cadaver in her garden with a flashlight.

I must have fallen asleep after that, because I awoke to the sound of Phoebe crying in her sleep. When I woke her, she denied it. "I was not crying. I most certainly was not."

In the morning, Phoebe refused to get up. Her father rushed into the room with two ties slung around his neck and his shoes in his hand. "Phoebe, you're late."

"I'm sick," she said. "I have a fever and a stomachache."

Her father placed his hand on her forehead, looked deep into her eyes and said, "I'm afraid you have to go to school."

"I'm sick. Honest," she said. "It might be cancer."

"Phoebe, I know you're worried, but there's nothing we can do but wait. We have to go on with things. We can't malinger."

"We can't what?" Phoebe said.

"Malinger. Here. Look it up." He tossed her the dictionary from her desk and tore down the hall.

"My mother is missing, and my father hands me a dictionary," Phoebe said. She looked up *malinger* and read the definition: "'To pretend to be ill in order to escape duty or work.'" She slammed the book shut. "I am *not* malingering."

Prudence was in a frenzy. "Where is my white blouse? Phoebe, have you seen—? I could have sworn—!" She pulled things out of her closet and flung them on the bed.

Phoebe reluctantly got dressed, pulling a wrinkled blouse and skirt from the closet. Downstairs, the kitchen table was bare. "No bowls of muesli," Phoebe said. "No glasses of orange juice or whole wheat toast." She touched a white sweater hanging on the back of a chair. "My mother's favorite white cardigan," she said. She snatched the sweater and waved it in front of her father. "Look at this! Would she leave this behind? Would she?"

He reached forward and touched its sleeve, rubbing the fabric between his fingers for a moment. "Phoebe, it's an old sweater." Phoebe put it on over her wrinkled blouse.

I was uneasy because everything that happened at Phoebe's that morning reminded me of when my mother left. For weeks, my father and I fumbled around like ducks in a fit. Nothing was where it was supposed to be. The house took on a life of its own, hatching piles of dishes and laundry and newspapers and dust. My father must have said "I'll be jiggered" three thousand times. The chickens were fidgety, the cows were skittish, and the pigs were sullen and glum. Our dog, Moody Blue, whimpered for hours on end.

When my father said that my mother was not coming back, I refused to believe it. I brought all her postcards down from my room and said, "She wrote me all these, she must be coming back." And just like Phoebe, who had waved her mother's sweater in front of her father, I had brought a chicken in from the coop: "Would Mom leave her favorite chicken?" I demanded. "She loves this chicken."

What I really meant was, "How can she not come back to *me*? She loves me."

At school, Phoebe slammed her books on her desk. Beth Ann said, "Hey, Phoebe, your blouse is a little wrinkled—"

"My mother's away," Phoebe said.

"I iron my own clothes now," Beth Ann said. "I even iron—"

To me, Phoebe whispered, "I think I'm having a genuine heart attack."

I thought about a baby rabbit that our dog, Moody Blue, caught and carried around—she was not actually lunching on the rabbit, just playing. I finally coaxed Moody Blue to drop it, and when I picked up the rabbit, its heart was beating faster than anything. Faster and faster it went, and then all of a sudden its heart stopped.

I took the rabbit to my mother. She said, "It's dead, Salamanca."

"It can't be dead," I said. "It was alive just a minute ago."

I wondered what would happen if all of a sudden Phoebe's heart beat itself out like the rabbit's, and she fell down and died right there at school. Her mother would not even know Phoebe was dead.

After homeroom, Mary Lou said to Phoebe, "Did I hear you say your mother is away—?"

Christy and Megan gathered around. "Is your mother on a business trip?" Christy said. "My mother's always going to Paris on business trips. So where is your mother? On a business trip?"

Phoebe nodded.

"Where did she go?" Megan said. "Tokyo? Saudi Arabia?"

Phoebe said, "London."

"Oh, London," Christy said. "My mother's been there."

Phoebe turned to me with a puzzled expression on her face. I think that she was surprised at what she had said, but I knew exactly why she had lied. It was easier sometimes. I had done this myself when people asked about my mother. "Don't worry, Phoebe," I said.

She snapped, "I am *not* worried."

I had done that too. Whenever anyone tried to console me about my mother, I had nearly chomped their heads off. I was a complete ornery old donkey. When my father would say, "You must feel terrible," I denied it. "I don't," I told him. "I don't feel anything at all." But I did feel terrible. I didn't want to wake up in the morning, and I was afraid to go to sleep at night.

By lunchtime, people were coming at Phoebe from all directions. "How long will your mother be in London?" Mary Lou asked. "Is she having tea with the queen?"

"Tell her to go to Convent Garden," Christy said. "My mother just loves Convent Garden."

"It's *Cov*ent Garden, cabbage-head," Mary Lou said.

"It isn't," Christy said. "I'm sure it's *Con*vent Garden."

After school, we walked home with Ben and Mary Lou. Phoebe wouldn't say a word. "Whatsa matter, Free Bee?" Ben asked. "Talk."

Out of the blue, I said, "Everyone has his own agenda." Ben tripped over the curb, and Mary Lou gave me a peculiar look. I kept hoping that Phoebe's mother would be home. Even though the door was locked, I kept hoping. "Are you sure you want me to come in?" I said. "Maybe you want to be alone."

Phoebe said, "I *don't* want to be alone. Call your dad and see if you can stay for dinner again."

Inside, Phoebe called, "Mom?" She walked through the house, looking in each room. "That's it," Phoebe said. "I'm going to search for clues, for evidence that the lunatic has been here and dragged my mother off." I wanted to tell her that she was just fishing in the air and that probably her mother had not been kidnapped, but I knew that Phoebe didn't want to hear it.

When my mother did not return, I imagined all sorts of things. Maybe she had cancer and didn't want to tell us and was hiding in Idaho. Maybe she got knocked on the head and had amnesia and was wandering around Lewiston, not knowing who she really was, or thinking she was someone else. My father said, "She does not have cancer, Sal. She does not have amnesia. Those are fishes in the air." But I didn't believe him. Maybe he was trying to protect her—or me.

Phoebe prowled through the house, examining the walls and carpet, searching for bloodstains. She found several suspicious spots and unidentifiable hair strands. Phoebe marked the spots with pieces of adhesive tape and collected the hairs in an envelope.

Prudence was in a lather when she came home. "I made it!" she said. "I made it!" She was jumping all about. "I made cheerleading!" When Phoebe reminded her that their mother had been kidnapped, Prudence said, "Oh Phoebe, Mom wasn't kidnapped." She stopped jumping and looked around the kitchen. "So what are we supposed to have for dinner?"

Phoebe rummaged around in the cupboards. Prudence opened the freezer compartment and said, "Look at this." For a terrible moment, I thought she had found some chopped-up body parts in there. Maybe, just maybe, Phoebe was right. Maybe a lunatic *had* done away with her mother. I couldn't look. I could hear Prudence moving things in the freezer. At least she wasn't screaming.

There were no body parts in the freezer. Instead, stacked neatly, were plastic containers, each with a note attached. "Broc-Len Cas, 350, 1 hr," Prudence read, and "Mac Che, 325, 45 min," on and on and on.

"What's Broc-Len Cas?" I said.

Phoebe pried open the lid. Inside was a green and yellow hardened mass. "Broccoli and lentil casserole," she said.

When their father came home and was surprised to see dinner on the table, Prudence showed him the freezer contents. "Hm," he said. At dinner, we all ate quietly.

"I don't suppose you've heard anything—from Mom?" Prudence asked her father.

"Not yet," he said.

"I think we should call the police," Phoebe said.

"Phoebe."

"I'm *serious*. I found some suspicious spots." Phoebe pointed toward two adhesive-taped areas beneath the dining room table.

"What's that tape doing down there?" he asked.

Phoebe explained about the potential blood spots.

"Blood?" Prudence said. She stopped eating.

Phoebe pulled out the envelope and emptied the hair strands on the table. "Strange hairs," Phoebe explained.

Prudence said, "Uck."

Mr. Winterbottom tapped his fork against his knife. Then he stood up, took Phoebe's arm, and said, "Follow me." He went to the refrigerator, opened the freezer compartment, and indicated the plastic containers. "If your mother had been kidnapped by a lunatic, would she have had time to prepare all these meals? Would she have been able to say, 'Excuse me, Mr. Lunatic, while I prepare ten or twenty meals for my family to eat while I am kidnapped?'"

"You don't care," Phoebe said. "Nobody cares. Everyone has his own idiot agenda."

I left shortly after dinner. Mr. Winterbottom was in his study, phoning his wife's friends to see if they had any idea of where she might have gone.

"At least," Phoebe said to me, "he's doing something, but I still think we should call the police."

As I left Phoebe's, the dead-leaf crackly voice of Margaret Cadaver called to me from her house next door. "Sal? Do you want to come in? Your father's here—we're having dessert. Join us."

My father appeared behind her. "Come on, Sal," he said. "Don't be a goose."

"I am not a goose," I said. "I already had dessert, and I'm going home to work on my English report."

My father turned to Margaret. "I'd better go with her. Sorry—"

Margaret didn't say anything. She just stood there as my father retrieved his jacket and joined me. I knew it was mean, but I felt as if I had won a little victory over Margaret Cadaver.

On the way home, when Dad asked if Phoebe's mother had come back yet, I said, "No. Phoebe thinks a lunatic has carried her off."

"A lunatic? Isn't that a bit farfetched?"

"That's what I thought at first, but you never

know, do you? I mean it *could* happen. There could actually be a lunatic who—"

"Sal."

I was going to explain about the nervous young man and the mysterious messages, but my father would call me a goose. Instead, I said, "How do you know that someone—not exactly a lunatic, but just someone—didn't make Mom go to Idaho? Maybe it was blackmail—"

"Sal. Your mother went because she wanted to go."

"We should have stopped her."

"A person isn't a bird. You can't cage a person."

"She shouldn't have gone. If she hadn't gone—"

"Sal, I'm sure she intended to come back." We had reached our house, but we didn't go in. We sat on the porch steps. Dad said, "You can't predict—a person can't foresee—you never know—"

He looked away, and I felt miserable right along with him. I apologized for being ornery and for upsetting him. He put his arm around me and we sat there together on the porch, two people being completely pitiful and lost.

23
THE BADLANDS

GRAMPS SAID, "HOW'S YOUR SNAKE LEG, GOOSE-berry?" He was worried about Gram, but less about her leg than her raspy breathing. "We'll stop in the Badlands, okay?" Gram merely nodded.

The closer we got to the Badlands, the more wicked were the whispers in the air: *Slow down, slow, slow, slow.* "Maybe we shouldn't go to the Badlands," I suggested.

"What? Not go? Of course we should go," Gramps said. "We're almost there. It's a national treasure."

My mother must have traveled on this road. What was she thinking about when she saw that sign? Or that one? When she reached this spot in the road?

My mother did not drive. She was terrified of cars. "I don't like all that speed," she said. "I like to be in control of where I'm going and how fast I'm going." When she said she was going all the way to Lewiston, Idaho, on a bus, my father and I were astonished.

I could not imagine why she had chosen Idaho. I thought perhaps she had opened an atlas and pointed a finger at any old spot, but later I learned that she had a cousin in Lewiston, Idaho. "I haven't seen her for fifteen years," my mother said, "and that's good because she'll tell me what I'm really like."

"I could tell you that, Sugar," my father said.

"No, I mean before I was a wife and a mother. I mean *underneath*, where I am Chanhassen."

After driving for so long through the flat South Dakota prairie, it was a shock to come upon the Badlands. It was as if someone had ironed out all the rest of South Dakota and smooshed all the hills and valleys and rocks into this spot. Right smack in the middle of flat plains were jagged peaks and steep gorges. Above was the high blue sky and below were the pink and purple and black rocks. You can stand right on the edge of the gorges and see down, down into the most treacherous ravines, lined with sharp, rough outcroppings. You expect to see human skeletons dangling here and there.

Gram tried to say, "Huzza, huzza," but she

could not breathe well. "Huz—huz—" she rasped. Gramps placed a blanket on the ground so that she could sit and look.

My mother sent two postcards from the Badlands. One of them said, "Salamanca is my left arm. I miss my left arm."

I told Gram and Gramps a story that my mother had told me about the high sky, which looked higher here than anywhere else I had been. Long ago, the sky was so low that you might bump your head on it if you were not careful, and so low that people sometimes disappeared right up into it. People got a little fed up with this, so they made long poles, and one day they all raised their poles and pushed. They pushed the sky as high as they could.

"And lookee there," Gramps said. "They pushed so good, the sky stayed put."

While I was telling this story, a pregnant woman stood nearby, dabbing at her face with a tissue. "That woman looks world-weary," Gramps said. He asked her if she would like to rest on our blanket.

"I'll go look around," I said. Pregnant women frightened me.

When my mother first told me she was pregnant, she added, "At last! We really are going to fill this house up with children." At first I didn't like the idea. What was wrong with having just me? My mother, father, and I were our own little unit.

As the baby grew inside her, my mother let me listen to its heartbeat and feel it kicking against her, and I started looking forward to seeing this baby. I hoped it would be a girl, and I would have a sister. Together, my father, my mother, and I decorated the nursery. We painted it sparkling white and hung yellow curtains. My father stripped an old dresser and repainted it. People gave us the tiniest baby clothes. We washed and folded each shirt, each jumpsuit, each sleeper. We bought fresh new cloth diapers because my mother liked to see diapers hanging on the line outside.

The one thing we could not do was settle on a name. Nothing seemed quite right. Nothing was perfect enough for this baby. My father seemed more worried about this than my mother. "Something will come to us," my mother said. "The perfect name will arrive in the air one day."

Three weeks before the baby was due, I was out in the woods beyond the farthest field. My father was in town on errands; my mother was scrubbing the floors. She said that scrubbing the floors made her back feel better. My father didn't like her to do this, but she insisted. My mother was not a fragile, sickly woman. It was normal for her to do this sort of thing.

In the woods, I climbed an oak, singing my mother's song: *Oh, don't fall in love with a sailor boy, a sailor boy, a sailor boy*—I climbed higher and higher. *Don't fall in love with a sailor boy*—

Then the branch I stepped on snapped, and I grabbed out at another, but it was dead and came away in my hands. I fell down, down, as if I were in slow motion. I saw leaves. I knew I was falling.

When I came to, I was on the ground with my face pressed into the dirt. My right leg was twisted beneath me and when I tried to move, it felt as if sharp needles were shooting all up and down my leg. I tried to drag myself across the ground, but the needles shot up to my brain and made everything black. There was a walloping buzzing in my head.

I must have passed out again, because the next time I opened my eyes, the woods were darker and the air was cooler. I heard my mother calling. Her voice was distant and faint, coming, I thought, from near the barn. I answered, but my voice was caught in my chest.

My mother found me and carried me back through the woods, across the fields, and down the long hill to the house. She called my grandparents to come take us to the hospital. It took forever just to get a cast, and by the time we got home we were all exhausted. My father felt awful that he had been away and fussed over both of us constantly.

The baby came that night. I heard my father telephoning the doctor. "She won't make it," he said. "It's happening now, right now."

On my new crutches, I tottered down the hall. My mother was sunk into the pillow, sweating and groaning. "Something's wrong," she said to my father. She saw me standing there and said, "You shouldn't watch. I don't think I'm very good at this."

In the hallway outside her room, I lowered myself to the floor. The doctor came. My mother screamed just once, one long, mournful wail, and then it was quiet.

When the doctor carried the baby out of the room, I asked to see it. It had a pale, bluish tinge and there were marks on its neck where the umbilical chord had strangled it. "It might have been dead for hours," the doctor told my father. "I just can't say exactly."

"Was it a boy or a girl?" I asked.

The doctor whispered his answer, "A girl."

I asked if I could touch her. She was still a little warm from being inside my mother. She looked so sweet and peaceful, all curled up, and I wanted to hold her, but the doctor said that was not a good idea. I thought maybe if I held her she would wake up.

My father looked shaken, but he didn't seem concerned about the baby anymore. He kept going in and touching my mother. He said to me, "It wasn't your fault, Sal—it wasn't because she carried you. You mustn't think that."

I didn't believe him. I hobbled into my mother's room and crawled up on the bed beside her. She was staring at the ceiling.

"Let me hold it," she said.

"Hold what?"

"The baby," she said. Her voice was odd and silly.

My father came in and she asked him for the baby. He leaned down and said, "I wish—I wish—"

"The baby," she said.

"It didn't make it," he said.

"I'll hold the baby," she said.

"It didn't make it," he repeated.

"It can't be dead," she said in that same singsong voice. "It was alive just a minute ago."

I slept beside her until I heard her calling my father. When he turned on the light, I saw the blood spread out all across the bed. It had soaked the sheets and the blanket; it had soaked into the white plaster of my cast.

An ambulance came and took her and my father away. Gram and Gramps came to stay with me. Gram took all the sheets and boiled them. She scrubbed the blood from my cast as best she could, but a dark pink stain remained.

My father came home from the hospital briefly the next day. "We should name the baby anyway," he said. "Do you have any suggestions?"

The name came to me from the air. "Tulip," I said.

My father smiled. "Your mother will like that. We'll bury the baby in the little cemetery near the aspen grove—where the tulips come up every spring."

My mother had two operations in the next two days. She wouldn't stop bleeding. Later, my mother said, "They took out all my equipment." She would not have any more babies.

☾

I sat on the edge of a gorge in the Badlands, looking back at Gram and Gramps and the pregnant woman on the blanket. I pretended that it was my mother sitting there and she would still have the baby and everything would be the way it was supposed to be. And then I tried to imagine my mother sitting here on her trip out to Lewiston, Idaho. Did all the people on the bus get out and walk around with her or did she sit by herself, like I was doing? Did she sit here in this spot and did she see that pink spire? Was she thinking about me?

I picked up a flat stone and sailed it across the gorge where it hit the far wall and plummeted down, down, careening off the jagged outcroppings. My mother once told me the Blackfoot story of Napi, the Old Man who created men and women. To decide if these new people should live forever or die, Napi selected a stone. "If the stone floats," he said, "you will live forever. If it sinks, you will die." Napi dropped the stone into the water. It sank. People die.

"Why did Napi use a stone?" I asked. "Why not a leaf?"

My mother shrugged. "If you had been there, you could have made the rock float," she said. She was referring to my habit of skipping stones across the water.

I picked up another rock and sailed it across the gorge, and this one, too, hit the opposite wall and fell down and down and down. It was not a river. It was a hole. What did I expect?

24
BIRDS OF SADNESS

AS WE WERE LEAVING THE BADLANDS, GRAMPS swore at a driver who cut us off. Usually when Gramps cussed like this, Gram threatened to go back to the egg man. I don't know that whole story, just that one time when Gramps was cussing up a storm, Gram ran off with the man who regularly bought eggs from Gramps. Gram stayed with the egg man for three days and three nights until Gramps came to get her and promised he wouldn't swear anymore.

I once asked Gram if she would really go back to the egg man if Gramps cussed too much. She said, "Don't tell your grandfather, but I don't mind a few hells and damns. Besides, that egg man snored to beat the band."

"So you didn't leave Gramps just because of the cussing?"

"Salamanca, I don't even remember why I did

that. Sometimes you know in your heart you love someone, but you have to go away before your head can figure it out."

That night we stayed at a motel outside of Wall, South Dakota. They had one room left, with only one bed in it, but Gramps was tired, so he said it would do. The bed was a king-size water bed. "Gol-dang," Gramps said. "Lookee there." When he pressed his hand on it, it gurgled. "Looks like we'll all have to float on this raft together tonight."

Gram flopped down on the bed and giggled. "Huz-huz," she said, in her raspy voice. She rolled into the middle. "Huz-huz." I lay down next to her, and Gramps tentatively sat down on the other side. "Whoa," he said. "I do believe this thing's alive." The three of us lay there sloshing around as Gramps turned this way and that. "Gol-darn," he said. Tears were streaming down Gram's face she was giggling so hard.

Gramps said, "Well, this ain't our marriage bed—"

That night I dreamed that I was floating down a river on a raft with my mother. We were lying on our backs looking up at the high sky. The sky moved closer and closer to us. There was a sudden popping sound and then we were up in the sky. Momma looked all around and said, "We can't be dead. We were alive just a minute ago."

In the morning, we set out for the Black Hills and Mt. Rushmore, hoping to be there by lunchtime. No sooner were we in the car than Gramps said, "So what happened to Peeby's mother and did Peeby get any more of those messages?"

"I hope everything turned out all right," Gram said. "I'm a little worried about Peeby."

On the day after Phoebe showed her father the suspicious spots and the unidentifiable hair strands, another message appeared: *You can't keep the birds of sadness from flying over your head, but you can keep them from nesting in your hair.* Phoebe brought the message to school to show me. "The lunatic again," she said.

"If he has already kidnapped your mother, why would he still be leaving messages?"

"They're clues," she said.

At school, people kept asking Phoebe about her mother's business trip to London. She tried to ignore them, but it wasn't always possible. She had to answer some of the time.

When Megan asked Phoebe what sights her mother had seen, Phoebe said, "Buckingham Palace—"

"Of course," Megan nodded knowingly.

"And Big Ben, and—" Phoebe was struggling. "Shakespeare's birthplace."

"But that's in Stratford-on-Avon," Megan said. "I thought your mother was in London. Stratford is miles away. Did she go on a day trip or something?"

"Yes, that's what she did. She went on a day trip."

Phoebe couldn't help it. She looked as if a whole family of the birds of sadness were nesting in her hair.

In English class, Ben had to give his mythology report. He was nervous. He explained that Prometheus stole fire from the sun and gave it to man. Zeus, the chief god, was angry at man and at Prometheus for taking some of his precious sun. As punishment, Zeus sent Pandora (a woman) to man. Then Zeus chained Prometheus to a rock and sent vultures down to eat Prometheus's liver. In Ben's nervousness, he mispronounced Prometheus, so what he actually said was that Zeus sent vultures down to eat porpoise's liver.

Mary Lou invited both me and Phoebe to dinner that night. When I phoned my father, he did not seem to mind, and I knew he wouldn't. All he said was, "That will be nice for you, Sal. Maybe I'll go eat over at Margaret's."

25
CHOLESTEROL

DINNER AT THE FINNEYS' WAS AN EXPERIENCE. When we arrived, Mary Lou's brothers were running around like crazed animals, jumping over the furniture and tossing footballs. Mary Lou's older sister, Maggie, was talking on the telephone and plucking her eyebrows at the same time. Mr. Finney was cooking something in the kitchen, with the help of four-year-old Tommy. Phoebe whispered, "I am not too optimistic about the possibilities of this meal."

When Mrs. Finney straggled in the door at six o'clock, Tommy and Dougie and Dennis tugged at various parts of her, all of them talking at once. "Look at this," and "Mom, Mom, Mom," and "Me first!" She made her way into the kitchen, trailing all three of them like a fishhook that has snagged a tangle of old tires and boots and other miscellaneous rubbish. She gave Mr. Finney a sloppy kiss on the lips, and he slipped a piece of cucumber into her mouth.

Mary Lou and I set the table, although I think it was largely a wasted effort. Everyone descended on the table in a chaotic flurry, knocking over glasses and sending forks onto the floor and picking up plates (which did not match, Phoebe pointed out to me) and saying, "That's my plate. I want the daisy plate," and "Give me the blue one! It's my turn for the blue plate."

Phoebe and I sat between Mary Lou and Ben. In the center of the table was a whomping platter of fried chicken. Phoebe said, "Chicken? Fried? I can't eat fried foods. I have a sensitive stomach." She glanced at the three pieces of chicken on Ben's plate. "You really shouldn't eat that, Ben. Fried foods aren't good for you. First of all, there's the cholesterol—"

Phoebe removed two pieces of chicken from Ben's plate and put them back on the serving platter. Mr. Finney coughed. Mrs. Finney said, "You're not going to eat the chicken then, Phoebe?"

Phoebe smiled. "Oh no, Mrs. Finney. I couldn't possibly. Actually, Mr. Finney shouldn't be eating it either. I don't know if you're aware of this, but men should really be careful about their cholesterol."

Mr. Finney stared down at his chicken. Mrs. Finney was rolling her lips around peculiarly. By this time, the beans had been passed to Phoebe. "Did you put butter on these beans, Mrs. Finney?"

"Yes, I did. Is there something wrong with butter?"

"*Cholesterol*," Phoebe said. "Cho-les-ter-ol. In the butter."

"Ah," Mrs. Finney said. "Cholesterol." She looked at her husband. "Be careful, dear. There's cholesterol on the beans."

I stared at Phoebe. I am sure I was not the only one in the room who wanted to strangle her.

Ben pushed his beans to one side of his plate. Maggie picked up a bean and examined it. When the potatoes came around, Phoebe explained that she was on a diet and could not eat starch. The rest of us looked glumly down at our plates. There was nothing at all on Phoebe's plate. Mrs. Finney said, "So what do you eat, Phoebe?"

"My mother makes special vegetarian meals. Low-calorie and no cholesterol. We eat a lot of salads and vegetables. My mother's an excellent cook."

She never mentioned the cholesterol in all those pies and brownies her mother made. I wanted to jump up and say, "Phoebe's mother has disappeared and that is why Phoebe is acting like a complete donkey," but I didn't.

Phoebe repeated, "A truly excellent cook."

"Marvelous," Mrs. Finney said. "And what do you propose to eat tonight?"

"I don't suppose you have any unadulterated vegetables?"

"Unadulterated?" Mrs. Finney said.

"It means unspoiled, without any butter or stuff added—"

"I know what it means, Phoebe," Mrs. Finney said.

"I can eat unadulterated vegetables. Or if you have any red bean salad handy—or stuffed cabbage leaves? Broccoli and lentil casserole? Macaroni and cheese? Vegetarian spaghetti?"

One by one, everyone at the table turned to stare at Phoebe. Mrs. Finney got up from the table and went into the kitchen. We heard her opening and closing cupboards. She returned to the doorway. "Muesli?" she asked Phoebe. "Can you eat muesli?"

Phoebe said, "Oh yes, I eat muesli. For breakfast."

Mrs. Finney disappeared again and returned

with a bowl of dried-up muesli and a bottle of milk.

"For dinner?" Phoebe asked. She gazed down at the bowl. "I usually eat it with yogurt on it—not milk," she said.

Mrs. Finney turned to Mr. Finney. "Dear, did you buy yogurt this week?"

"Blast it! How could I forget the yogurt?"

Phoebe ate her dried-up muesli without milk. All through dinner, I kept thinking of Bybanks, and what it was like when we went to my grandparents' house for dinner. There were always tons of people—relatives and neighbors—and lots of confusion. It was a friendly sort of confusion, and it was like that at the Finneys'. Tommy spilled two glasses of milk, Dennis punched Dougie, and Dougie punched him back. Maggie socked Mary Lou, and Mary Lou flipped a bean at her. Maybe this is what my mother had wanted, I thought. A house full of children and confusion.

On the way home, I said, "Didn't everyone seem unusually quiet after dinner?"

Phoebe said, "It was probably because of all that cholesterol sitting heavily on their stomachs."

I asked Phoebe if she wanted to spend the weekend at my house. I'm not sure why I did this.

It was an impulse. I had not yet invited anyone to my house. She said, "I guess. That is, if my mother is still—" She coughed. "Let's go ask my dad."

In the kitchen, her father was washing the dishes. He was wearing a frilly apron over his white shirt and tie. "You're supposed to rinse the soap off," Phoebe said. "And is that cold water you're using? You're supposed to use really, really hot water. To kill the germs."

He didn't look at Phoebe. I thought maybe he was embarrassed to be caught doing the dishes.

"You've probably washed that plate enough," Phoebe said. He had been rubbing it around and around with the dishcloth. He stopped and stared down at the plate. I could practically see the birds of sadness pecking at his head, but Phoebe was busy swatting at her own birds.

"Did you call all of Mom's friends?" Phoebe asked.

"Phoebe," he said. "I'm looking into it. I'm a little tired. Do you mind if we don't discuss this now?"

"But don't you think we should call the police?"

"Phoebe—"

"Sal wants to know if I can spend the weekend at her house."

"Of course," he said.

"But what if Mom comes back while I'm at Sal's? Will you call me? Will you let me know?"

"Of course."

"Or what if she telephones? Maybe I should stay home. I think I should be here if she calls."

"If she telephones, I'll have her call you at Sal's," he said.

"But if we don't have any news by tomorrow," Phoebe said, "we should definitely call the police. We've waited too long already. What if she's tied up somewhere and waiting for us to rescue her?"

At home that night, I was working on my mythology report when Phoebe called. She was whispering. When she went downstairs to say good night to her father, he was sitting in his favorite chair staring at the television, but the television wasn't on. If she did not know her father better, she would have thought he had been crying. "But my father never cries," she said.

26
SACRIFICES

THE WEEKEND WAS UNBELIEVABLY LONG. PHOEBE
arrived with her suitcase on Saturday morning. I
said, "Golly, Phoebe, are you planning to spend a
month here?" When I took her up to my room, she
asked if she was going to be sharing the room with
me. "Why no, Phoebe," I said. "We built a whole
new extension just for you."

"You don't have to be sarcastic," she said.

"I was only teasing, Phoebe."

"But there's only one bed."

"Good powers of observation, Phoebe."

"I thought you might sleep downstairs on the
couch. People usually try to make their guests
comfortable." She looked around my room. "We're
going to be a little crowded in here, aren't we?"

I did not answer. I did not bash her over the
head. I knew why she was acting this way. She sat
down on my bed and bounced on it a couple times.

"I guess I'll have to get used to your lumpy mattress, Sal. Mine is very firm. A firm mattress is much better for your back. That's why I have such good posture. The reason you slouch is probably because of this mattress."

"Slouch?" I said.

"Well, you do slouch, Sal. Look in the mirror sometime." She mashed on my mattress. "Don't you know anything about having guests? You're supposed to give your guests the *best* that you have. You're supposed to make some sacrifices, Sal. That's what my mother always says. She says, 'In life, you have to make some sacrifices.'"

"I suppose your mother made a great sacrifice when she took off," I said. I couldn't help it. She was really getting on my nerves.

"My mother didn't 'take off.' Someone kidnapped her. She is undergoing tremendous sacrifice at this very moment in time." She started unpacking. "Where shall I put my things?" When I opened up the closet, she said, "What a mess! Do you have some extra hangers? Am I supposed to leave my clothes jammed up in the suitcase all weekend? A guest is supposed to have the best. It is only courtesy, Sal. My mother says—"

"I know, I know—sacrifice."

Ten minutes later, Phoebe mentioned that she was getting a headache. "It might even be a migraine. My aunt's foot doctor used to get migraines, only they turned out not to be migraines at all. Do you know what they were?"

"What?" I said.

"A brain tumor."

"Really?" I said.

"Yes," Phoebe said. "In her brain."

"Well, of course it would be in her brain, Phoebe. I figured that out when you said it was a brain tumor."

"I don't think that's a particularly sympathetic way to speak to someone with a migraine or potential brain tumor."

In my book was a picture of a tree. I drew a round head with curly hair, put a rope around the neck, and attached it to that tree.

It went on and on like that. I hated her that day. I didn't care how upset she was about her mother, I really hated her, and I wanted her to leave. I wondered if this was how my father felt when I threw all those temper tantrums. Maybe he hated me for a while.

After dinner, we walked over to Mary Lou's. Mr. and Mrs. Finney were rolling around on the front lawn in a pile of leaves with Tommy and Dougie, and Ben was sitting on the porch. I sat down beside him while Phoebe went looking for Mary Lou.

Ben said, "Phoebe's driving you crazy, isn't she?" I liked the way he looked right in your eyes when he talked to you.

"Extensively," I said.

"I bet Phoebe is lonely."

I don't know what came over me, but I almost reached up and touched his face. My heart was thumping so loudly that I thought he would be able to hear it. I went into the house. From the back window, I watched Mrs. Finney climb a ladder placed against the garage. On the roof, she took off her jacket and spread it out. A few minutes later, Mr. Finney came around the back of the house and climbed up the ladder. He took off his jacket and spread it out next to her. He lay down on the roof and put his arm around her. He kissed her.

On the roof, in the wide open air, they lay there kissing each other. It made me feel peculiar. They reminded me of my parents, before the stillborn baby, before the operation.

Ben came into the kitchen. As he reached into

the cupboard for a glass, he stopped and looked at me. Again I had that odd sensation that I wanted to touch his face, right there on his cheek, in that soft spot. I was afraid my hand might just lift up and drift over to him if I was not careful. It was most peculiar.

"Guess where Mary Lou is?" Phoebe said when she came in. "She's with *Alex*. On a *date*."

I had never been on a date. Neither, I assumed, had Phoebe.

That night at my house, I pulled the sleeping bag out of the closet and spread it on the floor. Phoebe looked at it as if it were a spider. "Don't worry," I said, "I'll sleep in it." I crawled in and pretended to fall asleep immediately. I heard Phoebe get into bed.

A little later, my father came into the room. "Phoebe?" he said. "Is something the matter?"

"No," she said.

"I thought I heard someone crying. Are you okay?"

"Yes," she said.

"Are you sure?"

"Yes."

I felt bad for Phoebe. I knew I should get up and try to be nice, but I remembered when I had felt like that, and I knew that sometimes you just wanted to be alone with the birds of sadness. Sometimes you had to cry by yourself.

That night I dreamed that I was sitting on the grass peering through a pair of binoculars. Far off in the distance, my mother was climbing up a ladder. She kept climbing and climbing. It was a thumpingly tall ladder. She couldn't see me, and she never came down. She just kept on going.

27
PANDORA'S BOX

THE NEXT DAY, AS I WAS HELPING PHOEBE LUG HER suitcase home, I said, "Phoebe, I know you've been upset lately—"

"I have not been upset lately," she said.

"Sometimes, Phoebe, I like you a lot—"

"Why, thank you."

"—but sometimes, Phoebe, I feel like dumping your cholesterol-free body out the window."

She did not have a chance to respond, because we were at her house, and she was more interested in besieging her father with questions. "Any news? Did Mom come back? Did she call?"

"Sort of," he said. "She phoned Mrs. Cadaver—"

"Mrs. Cadaver? Whatever for? Why would she—"

"Phoebe, calm down. I don't know why she phoned Mrs. Cadaver. I haven't been able to speak to Mrs. Cadaver myself yet. She isn't home. She left a note here." He showed it to Phoebe: *Norma called to say she is okay.* Beneath Mrs. Cadaver's signature was a P.S. saying that Mrs. Cadaver would be away until Monday.

"I don't believe that Mom called Mrs. Cadaver. Mrs. Cadaver is making it up. Mrs. Cadaver probably killed her and chopped her up. I'm calling the police."

They had a huge argument, but at last Phoebe fizzled out. Her father said he had been calling everyone he could think of, to see if her mother had indicated where she might be going. He would continue calling tomorrow, he promised, and he would speak with Mrs. Cadaver. If he did not receive a letter—or a direct phone call—from her mother by Wednesday, he would call the police.

Phoebe came out on the porch with me as I was leaving. She said, "I've made a decision. I'm going to call the police. I might even go to the police station. I don't have to wait until Wednesday. I can go whenever I want."

That night she phoned me. She was whispering again. "It seems so quiet here. I don't know what is the matter with me. I was lying on my bed and I can't sleep. My bed's too hard."

On Monday, Phoebe gave her oral report on

Pandora. She began in a quivering voice. "For some reason, Ben already talked about my topic, Pandora, when he did his report on Prometheus. However, Ben made a few little mistakes about Pandora."

Everyone turned around to stare at Ben. "I did not," he said.

"Yes, you did." Phoebe's lip trembled. "Pandora was *not* sent to man as a *punishment*, but as a *reward*—"

"Was not," Ben said.

"Was too," Phoebe said. "Zeus decided to give man a present, since man seemed lonely down there on Earth, with only the animals to keep him company. So Zeus made a sweet and beautiful woman, and then Zeus invited all the gods to dinner. It was a very civilized dinner, with *matching plates*."

Mary Lou and Ben exchanged an eyebrow message.

"Zeus asked the gods to give the woman presents—to make her feel like a *welcome guest*." Phoebe glanced at me. "They gave her wonderful things: a fancy shawl, a silver dress, beauty—"

Ben interrupted. "I thought you said she was already beautiful."

"They gave her *more* beauty. Are you satisfied?" Her lip was no longer trembling, but she was blushing. "The gods also gave her the ability to sing, the power of persuasion, a gold crown, flowers, and many truly wonderful things such as that. Because of all these gifts, Zeus named her Pandora, which means 'the gift of all.'"

Phoebe was getting into it. "There were two other gifts that I have not mentioned yet. One of them was curiosity. That is why all women are curious, by the way, because it was a gift given to the very first woman."

Ben said, "I wish she had been given the gift of silence."

"Last, there was a beautiful box, covered in gold and jewels, and this is very important—she was forbidden to open the box."

Ben said, "Then why did they give it to her?"

He was beginning to irritate Phoebe, you could tell. She said, "That's what I'm telling you. It was a *present.*"

"But why did they give her a present that she couldn't open?"

"I-do-not-know. It's just in the story. As I was *saying*, Pandora was not supposed to open the box, but because she had been given so much curiosity, she really, really, really wanted to know what was inside, so one day she opened the box."

"I knew it," Ben said. "I knew she was going to open the box the minute that you said she was not supposed to open it."

"Inside the box were all the evils in the world, such as hatred, envy, plagues, sickness, and cholesterol. There were brain tumors and sadness, lunatics and kidnapping and murders"—she glanced at Mr. Birkway before rushing on—"and all that kind of thing. Pandora tried to close the lid when she saw all the horrible things that were coming out of it, but she could not get it closed, and that is why there are all these evils in the world. There was only one good thing in the box."

"What was it?" Ben asked.

"As I was *about* to explain, the only good thing in the box was Hope, and that is why, even though there are many evils in the world, there is still a little hope." She held up a picture of Pandora opening up the box and a whole shebang of gremlins floating out. Pandora looked frightened.

That night I kept thinking about Pandora's box. I wondered why someone would put a good thing such as Hope in a box with sickness and kidnapping and murder. It was fortunate that it was there, though. If not, people would have the birds of sadness nesting in their hair all the time, because of nuclear war and the greenhouse effect and bombs and stabbings and lunatics.

There must have been another box with all the good things in it, like sunshine and love and trees and all that. Who had the good fortune to open that one, and was there one bad thing down there in the bottom of the good box? Maybe it was Worry. Even when everything seems fine and good, I worry that something will go wrong and change everything.

My mother, my father, and I all seemed fine and happy at our house until the baby died. Could you actually say that the baby died, since it had never breathed? Did its birth and death occur at the same moment? Could you die *before* you were born?

Phoebe's family had *not* seemed fine, even before the arrival of the lunatic and the messages, and the disappearance of Mrs. Winterbottom. I knew that Phoebe was convinced that her mother was kidnapped because it was impossible for Phoebe to imagine that her mother could leave for any other reason. I wanted to call Phoebe and say that maybe her mother had gone looking for something, maybe her mother was unhappy, maybe there was nothing Phoebe could do about it.

When I told this part to Gram and Gramps, Gramps said, "You mean it had nothing to do with Peeby?" They looked at each other. They didn't say anything, but there was something in that look that suggested I had just said something important. For the first time, it occurred to me that maybe my mother's leaving had nothing whatsoever to do with me. It was separate and apart. We couldn't own our mothers.

On that night after Phoebe had given her Pandora report, I thought about the Hope in Pandora's box. Maybe when everything seemed sad and miserable, Phoebe and I could both hope that something might start to go right.

28
THE BLACK HILLS

When we saw the first sign for the Black Hills, the whispers changed and once again commanded, *rush, hurry, rush*. We had spent too long in South Dakota. There were only two days left and a long way to go.

"Maybe we should skip the Black Hills," I said.

"What?" Gramps said. "Skip the Black Hills? Skip Mount Rushmore? We can't do that."

"But today's the eighteenth. It's the fifth day."

"Do we have a deadline someone didn't tell me about?" Gramps asked. "Heck, we've got all the time in the—" Gram gave him a look. "I've just gotta see these Black Hills," Gramps said. "We'll be quick about it, chickabiddy."

The whispers walloped me: *rush, rush, rush*. I knew we wouldn't make it to Idaho in time. I thought about sneaking off while Gram and Gramps were looking at the Black Hills. Maybe I could hitch a ride with someone who drove fast, but the thought of someone speeding, careening around curves—especially the snaking curves down into Lewiston, Idaho, which I had heard so much about—when I thought about that, it made me dizzy and sick.

"Heck," Gramps said, "I oughta turn this wheel over to you, chickabiddy. All this driving is making me crazy as a loon."

He was only joking, but he knew I could drive. He had taught me to drive his old pickup truck when I was eleven. We used to ride around on the dirt roads on their farm. I drove, and he smoked his pipe and told stories. He said, "You're a helluva driver, chickabiddy, but don't you tell your Momma I taught you. She'd thrash me half to death."

I used to love to drive that old green pickup truck. I dreamed about turning sixteen and getting my license, but then when Momma left, something happened to me. I became afraid of things I had never been afraid of before, and driving was one of these things. I didn't even like to *ride* in cars, let alone drive the truck.

The Black Hills were not really black. Pines covered the hills, and maybe at dusk they looked black, but when we saw them at midday, they were dark green. It was an eerie sight, all those rolling dark hills. A cool wind blew down through the pines, and the trees swished secrets among them.

My mother had always wanted to see the Black Hills. It was one of the sights she was most looking forward to on her trip. She used to tell me about the Black Hills, which were sacred to the Sioux Indians. It was their Holy Land, but white settlers took it as their own. The Sioux are still fighting for their land. I half expected a Sioux to stop our car from entering, and the thing is, I would have been on his side. I would have said, "Take it. It's yours."

We drove through the Black Hills to Mt. Rushmore. At first we didn't think we were in the right place, but then, jing-bang, it was right before us. There, high up on a cliff face, were the sixty-foot-tall faces of Washington, Jefferson, Lincoln, and Teddy Roosevelt, carved right into the rock, staring somberly down on us.

It was fine seeing the presidents, I've got nothing against the presidents, but you'd think the Sioux would be mighty sad to have those white faces carved into their sacred hill. I bet my mother was upset. I wondered why whoever carved them couldn't have put a couple Indians up there too.

Gram and Gramps seemed disappointed as

well. Gram didn't even want to get out of the car, so we didn't stay long. Gramps said, "I've had enough of South Dakota, how about you, chick-abiddy? How about you, gooseberry? Let's get a move on."

By late afternoon, we were well into Wyoming, and I added up the miles left to go. Maybe we could make it, just maybe. Then Gramps said, "I hope nobody minds if we stop at Yellowstone. It would be a sin to miss Yellowstone."

Gram said, "Is that where Old Faithful is? Oh, I would love to see Old Faithful." She looked back at me. "We'll hurry. Why, I bet we'll be in Idaho by the twentieth without any problem at all."

29
THE TIDE RISES

"DID PEEBY'S MOTHER CALL?" GRAM SAID. "DID she come home? Did Peeby phone the police? Oh, I hope this isn't a sad story."

Phoebe did go to the police. It was on the day that Mr. Birkway read us the poem about the tide and the traveler—a poem that upset both me and Phoebe, and I think it is what convinced her, finally, that she had to tell the police about her mother.

Mr. Birkway read a poem by Longfellow: "The Tide Rises, The Tide Falls." The way Mr. Birkway read this poem, you could hear the tide rising and falling, rising and falling. In the poem, a traveler is hurrying toward a town, and it is getting darker and darker, and the sea calls to the traveler. Then the waves "with their soft, white hands" wash out the traveler's footprints. The next morning,

The day returns, but nevermore
Returns the traveller to the shore,
And the tide rises, the tide falls.

Mr. Birkway asked for reactions to this poem. Megan said that it sounded soft and gentle, and it almost made her go to sleep.

"Gentle?" I said. "It's terrifying." My voice was shaking. "Someone is walking along the beach, and the night is getting black, and the person keeps looking behind him to see if someone is following, and a jing-bang wave comes up and pulls him into the sea."

"A murder," Phoebe said.

I went barreling on as if it was my poem and I was an expert. "The waves, with their 'soft, white hands' grab the traveler. They drown him. They kill him. He's gone."

Ben said, "Maybe he didn't drown. Maybe he just died, like normal people die."

Phoebe said, "He drowned."

I said, "It isn't normal to die. It isn't normal. It's terrible."

Megan said, "What about heaven? What about God?"

Mary Lou said, "God? Is He in this poem?"

Ben said, "Maybe dying could be normal *and* terrible."

When the bell rang, I raced out of the room. Phoebe grabbed me. "Come on," she said. From her locker, she took the evidence she had brought from home, and we both ran the six blocks to the police station. I am not exactly sure why I went along with Phoebe. Maybe it was because of that poem about the traveler, or maybe it was because I had begun to believe in the lunatic, or maybe it was because Phoebe was taking some action, and I admired her for it. I wished I had taken some action when my mother left. I was not sure what I could have done, but I wished I had done *something*.

Phoebe and I stood for five minutes outside the police station, trying to make our hearts slow down, and then we went inside and stood at the counter. On the other side of it, a thin man with big ears was writing in a black book.

"Excuse me," Phoebe said.

"I'll be right with you," he said.

"This is absolutely urgent. I need to speak to someone about a murder," Phoebe said.

He looked up quickly. "A murder?"

"Yes," Phoebe said. "Or possibly a kidnapping.

But the kidnapping might turn into a murder."

"Is this a joke?"

"No, it is not a joke," Phoebe said.

"Just a minute." He whispered to a plump woman in a dark blue uniform. She wore glasses with thick lenses. "Is this something you girls have read about in a book?" she asked.

"No, it is not," I said. That was a turning point, I think, when I came to Phoebe's defense. I didn't like the way the woman was looking at us—as if we were two fools. I wanted that woman to understand why Phoebe was so upset. I wanted her to believe Phoebe.

"May I ask who it is who has been kidnapped or possibly murdered?" the woman said.

Phoebe said, "My mother."

"Oh, your mother. Come along, then." Her voice was sugary and sweet, as if she was speaking to tiny children. We followed her to a room with glass partitions. An enormous man with a huge head and neck, and massive shoulders, sat behind the desk. His hair was bright red, and his face was covered in freckles. He did not smile when we entered. After the woman repeated what we had told her, he stared at us for a long time.

His name was Sergeant Bickle, and Phoebe

told him everything. She explained about her mother disappearing, and the note from Mrs. Cadaver, and Mrs. Cadaver's missing husband, and the rhododendron, and finally about the lunatic and the mysterious messages. At this point, Sergeant Bickle said, "What sort of messages?"

Phoebe was prepared. She pulled them out of her book bag and laid them on the desk in the order in which they had arrived. He read each one aloud.

Don't judge a man until you've walked two moons in his moccasins.

Everyone has his own agenda.

In the course of a lifetime, what does it matter?

You can't keep the birds of sadness from flying over your head, but you can keep them from nesting in your hair.

Sergeant Bickle looked up at the woman seated next to us, and the corners of his mouth twitched slightly. To Phoebe, he said, "And how do you think these are related to your mother's disappearance?"

"I don't know," she said. "That's what I want you to find out."

Sergeant Bickle asked Phoebe to spell Mrs. Cadaver's name. "It means corpse," Phoebe said. "Dead body."

"I know. Is there anything else?"

Phoebe pulled out the envelope with the unidentifiable hair strands. "Perhaps you could have these analyzed," she suggested.

Sergeant Bickle looked at the woman, and again the corners of his mouth twitched slightly. The woman removed her glasses and wiped the lenses.

They were not taking us seriously, and I felt my ornery donkey self waking up. I mentioned the potential blood spots that Phoebe had marked with adhesive tape.

"But my father removed the tape," Phoebe said.

Sergeant Bickle said, "I wonder if you would excuse me a few minutes?" He asked the woman to stay with us, and he left the room.

The woman asked Phoebe about school and

about her family. She had an awful lot of questions. I kept wondering where Sergeant Bickle had gone and when he was coming back. He was gone for over an hour. There were three framed pictures on Sergeant Bickle's desk, and I tried to lean forward to see them, but I couldn't. I was afraid the woman would think I was nosy.

Sergeant Bickle finally returned. Behind him was Phoebe's father. Phoebe looked extensively relieved, but I knew it was not a coincidence that her father was there.

"Miss Winterbottom," Sergeant Bickle said, "your father is going to take you and your friend home now."

"But—" Phoebe said.

"Mr. Winterbottom, we'll be in touch. And if you would like me to speak with Mrs. Cadaver—"

"Oh no," Mr. Winterbottom said. He looked embarrassed. "Really, that won't be necessary. I do apologize—"

We followed Mr. Winterbottom outside. In the car, he said nothing. I thought he might drop me off at my house, but he didn't. When we got to their house, the only thing he said was, "Phoebe, I'm going to go talk with Mrs. Cadaver. You and Sal wait here."

Mrs. Cadaver was unable to give him any more information about Phoebe's mother's call. All Mrs. Winterbottom had said was that she would phone soon.

"That's all?" Phoebe asked.

"Your mother also asked Mrs. Cadaver how you and Prudence were. Mrs. Cadaver told her that you and Prudence were fine."

"Well, I am *not* fine," Phoebe said, "and what does Mrs. Cadaver know anyway, and besides, Mrs. Cadaver is making the whole thing up. You should let the police talk to her. You should ask her about the rhododendron. You should find out who this lunatic is. Mrs. Cadaver probably hired him. You should—"

"Phoebe, your imagination is running away with you."

"It is not. Mom loves me, and she would not leave me without any explanation."

And then her father began to cry.

30
Breaking In

"GOL-DANG!" GRAMPS SAID. "WHAT A LOT OF BIRDS of sadness wing-dinging their way around Peeby's family."

Gram said, "You liked Peeby, didn't you, Salamanca?"

I did like Phoebe. In spite of all her wild tales and her cholesterol-madness and her annoying comments, there was something about Phoebe that was like a magnet. I was drawn to her. I was pretty sure that underneath all that odd behavior was someone who was frightened. And, in a strange way, she was like another version of me—she acted out the way I sometimes felt.

I do not think that Phoebe actually planned to break into Mrs. Cadaver's house, but as Phoebe was going to bed, she saw Mrs. Cadaver, in her nurse's uniform, get into her car and leave. Phoebe waited until her father was asleep, and then she phoned me. "You've got to come over," she said. "It's urgent."

"But Phoebe, it's late. It's dark."

"It's urgent, Sal."

Phoebe was waiting in front of Mrs. Cadaver's house. There were no lights on at Mrs. Cadaver's. Phoebe said, "Come on," and she started up the walk. I admit that I was reluctant. "I just want to take a quick look," she said. She crept up onto the porch and stood by the door. She listened, tapped twice, and turned the doorknob. The door was unlocked.

I don't think Phoebe intended to go inside, but she did, and I followed. We stood in the dark hallway. In the room to the right, a shaft of light from the streetlamp came in through the window. We went into that room. We both nearly leaped through the window when someone said, "Sal?" I started backing toward the door.

"It's a ghost," Phoebe said.

"Come here," the voice said.

As my eyes adjusted to the dim light, I could see someone huddled in a chair in the far corner. When I saw the cane, I was relieved. "Mrs. Partridge?"

"Come over here," she said. "Who's that with you? Is that Phoebe?"

Phoebe said, "Yes." Her voice was high and quivery.

"I was just sitting here reading," Mrs. Partridge said.

"Isn't it awfully dark in here?" I said, bumping a table.

Mrs. Partridge laughed her wicked laugh. "It's always dark in here. I don't need lights, but you can turn some on if you want to."

As I stumbled around looking for a lamp, Phoebe stood, frozen, near the doorway. "There," I said. "That's much better." Mrs. Partridge was sitting in a big, overstuffed chair. She was wearing a purple bathrobe and pink slippers with floppy bunny ears at the toes. On her lap was a book, her fingers resting on the page. "Is it Braille?" I asked, waving at Phoebe to come into the room. I was afraid she was going to run out and leave me.

Mrs. Partridge handed me the book, and I slid my fingers over the raised bumps. "How did you know it was us?" I asked.

"I just knew," she said. "Your shoes make a particular sound and you have a particular smell."

"What's the name of this book? What's it about?"

Mrs. Partridge said, "*Murder at Midnight.* It's a mystery."

Phoebe said, "Erp," and looked around the room.

Each time I went into that house I noticed new things. It was a scary place. The walls were lined with shelves crammed with old musty books. On the floor were three rugs with dark, swirly patterns of wild beasts in forests. Two chairs were covered in similar ghastly designs. A sofa was draped in a bear skin.

On the wall behind the couch were two thumpingly grim African masks. The mouths on the masks were wide open, as if in the midst of a scream. Everywhere you looked there was something startling: a stuffed squirrel, a kite in the shape of a dragon, a wooden cow with a spear piercing its side.

"Goodness," Phoebe said. "What a lot of—of—unusual things." She knelt to examine a spot on the floor.

"What's the matter?" Mrs. Partridge said.

Phoebe jumped up. "Nothing. Nothing whatsoever."

"Did I drop something on the floor?" Mrs. Partridge asked.

"No. Nothing whatsoever on the floor," Phoebe

said. Leaning against the back of the sofa was an enormous sword. Phoebe examined the blade.

"Careful you don't cut yourself," Mrs. Partridge said.

Phoebe stepped back. Even I found this unsettling, that Mrs. Partridge could see what Phoebe was doing even though she couldn't actually *see* her.

Mrs. Partridge said, "Isn't this a grandiful room? Grandiful—and a little peculible, too, I suppose."

"Phoebe and I have to be going—" We backed toward the door.

"By the way," Mrs. Partridge said as we reached the doorway, "what was it you wanted?"

Phoebe looked at me and I looked at Phoebe. "We were just passing by," I said, "and we thought we would see how you were doing."

"That's nice," Mrs. Partridge said, patting her knees. "Oh, Phoebe, I think I met your brother."

Phoebe said, "I don't have a brother."

"Oh?" Mrs. Partridge tapped her head. "I guess this old noggin isn't as sharp as it used to be." As we left, she said, "Goodness, you girls stay up late."

Outside, Phoebe said, "I'll make a list of items which the police will want to investigate further: the sword, the suspicious spot on the floor, and several hair strands which I picked up."

"Phoebe, you know when you said that your mother would never leave without an explanation? Well, she might. A person—a mother—might do that."

Phoebe said, "*My* mother wouldn't. *My* mother loves me."

"But she might love you and still not have been *able* to explain." I was thinking about the letter my mother left me. "Maybe it would be too painful for her to explain. Maybe it would seem too permanent."

"I don't know what in the world you are talking about."

"She might not come back, Phoebe—"

"Shut up, Sal."

"She might not. I just think you should be prepared—"

"She is too coming back. You don't know what you're talking about. You're being horrid." Phoebe ran into the house.

When I got home and had crept up to my room, I remembered how Phoebe had shown me some things in her room that reminded her of her mother: a handmade birthday card, a photograph of Phoebe and her mother, and a bar of lavender soap. When Phoebe pulled a blouse out of the closet, she said she could see her mother standing at the ironing board smoothing the blouse with her hand. The wall opposite Phoebe's bed was painted violet. She said, "My mother painted it last summer while I painted the trim at the bottom."

And I knew exactly what Phoebe was doing and exactly why. I had done the same things when my mother left. My father was right: my mother did haunt our house in Bybanks, and the fields and the barn. She was everywhere. You couldn't look at a single thing without being reminded of her.

When we moved to Euclid, one of the first things I did was to unpack gifts my mother had given me. On the wall, I tacked the poster of the red hen which my mother had given me for my fifth birthday, and the drawing of the barn she had given me for my last birthday. On my desk were pictures of her and cards from her. On the bookshelf, the wooden animals and books were presents from her.

Sometimes, I would walk around the room and look at each of these things and try to remember exactly the day she had given them to me. I tried to picture what the weather was like and what room we were in and what she was wearing and what precisely she had said. This was not a game. It was a necessary, crucial thing to do. If I did not have these things and remember these occasions, then she might disappear forever. She might never have been.

In my bureau were three things of hers that I had taken from her closet after she left: a red, fringed shawl; a blue sweater; and a yellow-flowered cotton dress that was always my favorite. These things had her smell on them.

Once, before she left, my mother said that if you visualize something happening, you can make it happen. For example, if you are about to run a race, you visualize yourself running the race and crossing the finish line first, and presto! When the time comes, it really happens. The only thing I did not understand was what if *everyone* visualized himself winning the race?

Still, when she left, this is what I did. I visualized her reaching for the phone. Then I visualized her dialing the phone. I visualized our phone number clicking through the wires. I visualized the phone ringing.

It did not ring.

I visualized her riding the bus back to Bybanks. I visualized her walking up the driveway. I visualized her opening the door.

It did not happen.

While I was thinking about all of this that night after Phoebe and I crept into Mrs. Cadaver's house, I also thought about Ben. I had the sudden urge to run over to the Finneys and ask him where his own mother was, but it was too late. The Finneys would be asleep.

Instead, I lay there thinking of the poem about the traveler, and I could see the tide rising and falling, and those horrid white hands snatching the traveler. How could it be normal, that traveler dying? And how could such a thing be normal *and* terrible both at the same time?

I stayed awake the whole night. I knew that if I closed my eyes, I would see the tide and the white hands. I thought about Mr. Winterbottom crying. That was the saddest thing. It was sadder than seeing my own father cry, because my father is the sort of person you expect might cry if he was terribly upset. But I had never, ever, expected Mr. Winterbottom—stiff Mr. Winterbottom—to cry. It was the first time I realized that he actually *cared* about Mrs. Winterbottom.

As soon as it was daylight, I phoned Phoebe. "Phoebe, we've got to find her."

"That's what I've been telling you," she said.

31
THE PHOTOGRAPH

THE NEXT DAY WAS MOST *PECULIBLE*, AS MRS. PARtridge would say.

Phoebe arrived at school with another message, which she had found on her porch that morning: *We never know the worth of water until the well is dry*. "It's a clue," Phoebe said. "Maybe my mother is hidden in a well."

I walked straight into Ben when I went to my locker. That grapefruit aroma was in the air. "You've got something on your face," he said. With soft, warm fingers he rubbed the side of my face. "It's probably your breakfast."

I don't know what came over me. I was going to kiss him. I leaned forward just as he turned around and slammed the door of his locker. My lips ended up pressed against the cold, metal locker.

"You're weird, Sal," he said.

Kissing was thumpingly complicated. Both people had to be in the same place at the same time, and both people had to remain still so that the kiss ended up in the right place. But I was relieved that my lips ended up on the cold metal locker. I could not imagine what had come over me, or what might have happened if the kiss had landed on Ben's mouth. It was a shivery thing to consider.

I made it through the rest of my classes without losing control of my lips.

Mr. Birkway sailed into class carrying our journals. I had forgotten all about them. He was leaping all over the place exclaiming, "Dynamite! Unbelievable! Incredible!" He said he couldn't wait to share the journals with the class.

Mary Lou Finney said, "*Share* with the *class*?"

Mr. Birkway said, "Not to worry! Everyone has something magnificent to say. I haven't read through every page yet, but I wanted to share some of these passages with you right away."

People were squirming all over the room. I was trying to remember what I had written. Mary Lou leaned over to me and said, "Well, I'm not worried. I wrote a special note in the front of mine distinctly asking him not to read it. Mine was private."

Mr. Birkway smiled at each nervous face. "You

needn't worry," he said. "I'll change any names that you've used, and I'll fold this piece of yellow paper over the cover of whichever journal I'm reading, so that you won't know whose it is."

Ben asked if he could go to the bathroom. Christy said she felt sick and begged to see the nurse. Phoebe asked me to touch her forehead because she was pretty sure she had a fever. Usually Mr. Birkway would let people go to the bathroom or to the nurse, but this time he said, "Let's not malinger!" He picked up a journal, slipping the yellow paper over it before anyone had a chance to examine the cover for clues as to its author's identity. Everyone took a deep breath. You could see people poised nervously, waiting as tensely as if Mr. Birkway was going to announce someone's execution. Mr. Birkway read:

> *I think that Betty* [he changed the name, you could tell, because there was no Betty in our school] *will go to hell because she always takes the Lord's name in vain. She says "God!" every five seconds.*

Mary Lou Finney was turning purple. "Who

wrote that?" she said. "Did you, Christy? I'll bet you did."

Christy stared down at her desk.

"I do not say 'God!' every five seconds. I do not. And I am not going to hell. Omnipotent—that's what I say now. I say, *Omnipotent*! And *Alpha and Omega!*"

Mr. Birkway was desperately trying to explain what he had enjoyed about that passage. He said that most of us are not aware that we might be using words—such as God!—that offend other people. Mary Lou leaned over to me and said, "Is he *serious*? Does he actually, really and truly believe that beef-brained Christy is troubled by my saying God?—which I do not, by the way, say anymore anyway."

Christy wore a pious look, as if God Himself had just come down from heaven to sit on her desk.

Mr. Birkway quickly selected another journal. He read:

> *Linda* [there was no Linda in our class either] *is my best friend. I tell her just about everything and she tells me EVERYTHING, even things*

*I do not want to know. Like what she
ate for breakfast and what her father
wears to bed and how much her
new sweater cost. Sometimes things
like that are just not interesting.*

Mr. Birkway liked this passage because it showed that even though someone might be our best friend, he or she could still drive us crazy. Beth Ann turned all the way around in her seat and sent wicked eyebrow-messages to Mary Lou.

Mr. Birkway flipped ahead in the same journal to another passage. He read:

*I think Jeremiah is pig-headed. His
skin is always pink and his hair is
always clean and shiny . . . but he is
really a jerk.*

I thought Mary Lou Finney was going to fall out of her chair. Alex was bright, bright pink. He looked at Mary Lou as if she had recently plunged a red hot stake into his heart. Mary Lou said, "No—I—no, it isn't what you think—I—"

Mr. Birkway liked this passage because it showed conflicting feelings about someone.

"I'll say it does," Alex said.

The bell rang. First, you could hear sighs of relief from the people whose journals had not been read, and then people started talking a mile a minute. "Hey, Mary Lou, look at Alex's pink skin," and "Hey Mary Lou, what *does* Beth Ann's father wear to bed?"

Beth Ann was standing one inch away from Mary Lou's face. "I do not talk on and on," Beth Ann said, "and that wasn't very nice of you to mention that, and I do not tell you everything, and the only reason I ever mentioned what my father wore to bed was because we were talking, if you will recall, about men's bathing suits being more comfortable than women's and—" On and on she went.

Mary Lou was trying to get across the room to Alex, who was standing there as pink as can be. "Alex!" she called. "Wait! I wrote that *before*—wait—"

It was a jing-bang of a mess. I was glad I had to get out of there. Phoebe and I were going to the police again.

We got in to see Sergeant Bickle right away. Phoebe slapped the newest message about the water in the well onto his desk, dumped the hairs which she had collected at Mrs. Cadaver's house on top of the message, and then placed her list of "Further Items to Investigate" on top of that.

Sergeant Bickle frowned. "I don't think you girls understand."

Phoebe went into a rage. "You idiot," she said. She scooped up the message, the hairs, and her list and stormed out of the office.

Sergeant Bickle followed her while I waited, thinking he would bring Phoebe back and calm her down. I looked at the photographs on his desk, the ones I had not been able to see the day before. In one was Sergeant Bickle and a friendly-looking woman—his wife, I supposed. The second picture was of a shiny black car. The third picture was of Sergeant Bickle, the woman, and a young man— their son, I figured. I looked closer.

I recognized the son. It was the lunatic.

32
CHICKEN AND BLACKBERRY KISSES

GRAMPS BARRELED THROUGH WYOMING LIKE A house afire. We snaked through winding roads where the trees leaned close, rustling *rush, rush, rush, rush, rush*. The road curved alongside rivers that rolled and gabbled *hurry, hurry, hurry*.

It was late when we arrived at Yellowstone. All we got to see that evening was a hot spring. We walked on boardwalks placed across the bubbling mud ("Huzza, huzza!" Gram said), and we stayed at the Old Faithful Inn in a Frontier Cabin. I'd never seen Gram so excited. She could not wait for the next morning. "We're gonna see Old Faithful," she said, over and over.

"It won't take too very long, will it?" I said, and I felt like a mule saying it, because Gram was so looking forward to it.

"Don't you worry, Salamanca," Gram said.

"We'll just watch that old geyser blow and then we'll hit the road."

I prayed all night long to the elm tree outside. I prayed that we would not get in an accident, that we would get to Lewiston, Idaho, in time for my mother's birthday, and that we would bring her home. Later I would realize that I had prayed for the wrong things.

That night, Gram was so excited that she could not sleep. She rambled on about all sorts of things. She said to Gramps, "Remember that letter from the egg man that you found under the mattress?"

"Of course I remember. We had a wing-ding of an argument over it. You told me you had no dang idea how it got there. You said the egg man must've slipped into the bedroom and put it there."

"Well, I want you to know that I put it there."

"I know that," Gramps said. "I'm not a complete noodle."

"It's the only love letter anybody ever wrote me," Gram said. "You never wrote me any love letters."

"You never told me you wanted one."

To me, Gram said, "Your grandfather nearly killed the egg man over that letter."

"Hell's bells," Gramps said. "He wasn't worth killing."

"Maybe not, but Gloria was."

"Ah yes," Gramps said, placing his hand on his heart and pretending to swoon, "Gloria!"

"Cut that out," Gram said, rolling over on her side. "Tell me about Peeby. Tell me that story, but don't make it too awfully sad." She folded her hands on her chest. "Tell me what happened with the lunatic."

When I saw the picture of the lunatic on Sergeant Bickle's desk, I tore out of that office faster than lightning. I ran past Sergeant Bickle standing in the parking lot. No sign of Phoebe. I ran all the way to her house. As I passed Mrs. Cadaver's house, Mrs. Partridge called to me from her porch.

"You're all dressed up," I said. "Going somewhere?"

"Oh yes," she said. "I'm redible." She tottered down the steps, swinging her cobra cane in front of her.

"Are you walking?" I asked.

She reached down and touched her legs. "Isn't that what you call it when you move your legs like I'm doing?"

"No, I meant are you walking to wherever you're going?"

"Oh no, it's much too far for these legs. Jimmy's coming. He'll be here any minute." A car pulled up in front of the house. "There he is," she said. She called out to the driver, "I'm redible. I said I would be, and here I am."

The driver leaped out of the car. "Sal?" he said. "I had no idea you two were neighbors." It was Mr. Birkway.

"We're not," I said. "It's Phoebe who is the neighbor—"

"Is that right?" he said, opening the car door for Mrs. Partridge. "Come on, Mom. Let's get a move on."

"Mom?" I said. I looked at Mrs. Partridge. "This is your son?"

"Why, of course," Mrs. Partridge said. "This is my little Jimmy."

"But he's a Birkway—?"

Mrs. Partridge said, "I was a Birkway once. Then I was a Partridge. I'm still a Partridge."

"Then who is Mrs. Cadaver?" I said.

"My little Margie," she said. "She was a Birkway too. Now she's a Cadaver."

I said to Mr. Birkway, "Mrs. Cadaver is your sister?"

"We're twins," Mr. Birkway said.

When they had driven away, I knocked at Phoebe's door, but there was no answer. At home, I dialed Phoebe's number over and over. No answer.

The next day at school, I was relieved to see Phoebe. "Where were you?" I said. "I have something to tell you—"

She turned away. "I don't want to talk about it," she said. "I do not wish to discuss it."

I couldn't figure out what was the matter with her. It was a terrible day. We had tests in math and science. At lunch, Phoebe ignored me. Then came English.

Mr. Birkway skipped into the room. People were gnawing on their fingers and tapping their feet and wriggling around and generally getting ulcers, wondering if Mr. Birkway was going to read from the journals. I stared at him. He and Margaret Cadaver were twins? Was that possible? The most disappointing part of that piece of knowledge was that he was not going to fall in love with Mrs. Cadaver and marry her and take her away.

Mr. Birkway opened a cupboard, pulled out the journals, slipped the yellow paper over the cover of one and read:

This is what I like about Jane. She is smart, but doesn't act like she knows everything. She is cute. She smells good. She is cute. She makes me laugh. She is cute.

I got a prickly feeling up and down my arms. I wondered if Ben had written this about me, but then I realized that Ben didn't even know me when he wrote his journal. A little buzz was going around the room as people shifted in their seats. Christy was smiling, Megan was smiling, Beth Ann was smiling, Mary Lou was smiling. Every girl in the room was smiling. Each girl thought that this had been written about her.

I looked carefully at each of the boys. Alex was gazing nonchalantly at Mr. Birkway. Then I saw Ben. He was sitting with his hands over his ears, staring down at his desk. The prickly feeling traveled all the way up to my neck and then went skipping down my spine. He did write that, but he did not write it about me.

Mr. Birkway exclaimed, "Ah love, ah life!" Sighing, he pulled out another journal and read:

Jane doesn't know the first thing

about boys. She once asked me what kisses taste like, so you could tell she hadn't ever kissed anyone. I told her that they taste like chicken, and she believed me. She is so dumb sometimes.

Mary Lou Finney jumped out of her chair. "You cabbage-head," she said to Beth Ann. "You beef brain." Beth Ann wound a strand of hair around her finger. Mary Lou said, "I did *not* believe you, and I do know what they taste like, and it isn't chicken."

Ben drew a cartoon of two stick-figures kissing. In the air over their heads was a cartoon bubble with a chicken saying, "Bawk, bawwwk, bawwwk."

Mr. Birkway turned a few pages in the same journal and read:

I hate doing this. I hate to write. I hate to read. I hate journals. I especially hate English where teachers only talk about idiot symbols. I hate that idiot poem about the snowy woods, and I hate it when people say the woods symbolize death or

beauty or sex or any old thing you
want. I hate that. Maybe the woods
are just woods.

Beth Ann stood up. "Mr. Birkway," she said, "I do hate school, I do hate books, I do hate English, I do hate symbols, and I most especially hate these idiot journals."

There was a hush in the room. Mr. Birkway stared at Beth Ann for a minute, and in that minute, I was reminded of Mrs. Cadaver. For that brief time, his eyes looked just like hers. I was afraid he was going to strangle Beth Ann, but then he smiled and his eyes became friendly enormous cow eyes once again. I think he hypnotized her, because Beth Ann sat down slowly. Mr. Birkway said, "Beth Ann, I know exactly how you feel. Exactly. I love this passage."

"You do?" she said.

"It's so honest."

I had to admit, you couldn't get more honest than Beth Ann telling her English teacher that she hated symbols and English and idiot journals.

Mr. Birkway said, "I used to feel exactly like this. I could not understand what all the fuss was about symbols." He rummaged around in his desk.

"I want to show you something." He was pulling papers out and flinging them around. Finally, he held up a picture. "Ah, here it is. Dynamite! What is this?" he asked Ben.

Ben said, "It's a vase. Obviously."

Mr. Birkway held the drawing in front of Beth Ann, who looked as if she might cry. Mr. Birkway said, "Beth Ann, what do you see?" A little tear dropped down on her cheek. "It's okay, Beth Ann, what do *you* see?"

"I don't see any idiot vase," she said. "I see two people. They're looking at each other."

"Right," Mr. Birkway said. "Bravo!"

"I'm right? Bravo?"

Ben said, "Huh? Two people?" I was thinking the same thing myself. What two people?

Mr. Birkway said to Ben, "And you were right, too. Bravo!" He asked everyone else, "How many see a vase?" About half the class raised their hands. "And how many see two faces?" The rest of the class raised their hands.

Then Mr. Birkway pointed out how you could see both. If you looked only at the white part in the center, you could clearly see the vase. If you looked only at the dark parts on the side, you could see two profiles. The curvy sides of the vase became the outline of the two heads facing each other.

Mr. Birkway said that the drawing was a bit like symbols. Maybe the artist only intended to draw a vase, and maybe some people look at this picture and see only that vase. That is fine, but if some people look at it and see faces, what is wrong with that? It *is* faces to that person who is looking at it. And, what is even more magnificent, you might see *both*.

Beth Ann said, "Two for your money?"

"Isn't it interesting," Mr. Birkway said, "to find both? Isn't it interesting to discover that snowy woods could be death *and* beauty *and* even, I suppose, *sex*? Wow! Literature!"

"Did he say *sex*?" Ben said, copying the drawing.

I thought Mr. Birkway was finished with the journals for that day, but he made a great show of closing his eyes and pulling something from near the bottom of the stack.

> *She popped the blackberries into her mouth. Then she looked all around—*

It was mine. I could hardly bear it.

She took two steps up to the maple tree and threw her arms around it, and kissed it.

People were giggling.

. . . I thought I could detect a small dark stain, as from a blackberry kiss.

Ben looked at me from across the room. After Mr. Birkway read about my mother's blackberry kiss, he read about how I kissed the tree and how I have kissed all different kinds of trees since then and how each tree has a special taste all its own, and mixed in with that taste is the taste of blackberries.

By now, because both Ben and Phoebe were staring at me, everyone else stared too. "She kisses *trees?*" Megan said. I might have died right then and there, if Mr. Birkway had not immediately picked up another journal. He stabbed his finger into the middle of the page and read:

I am very concerned about Mrs.—

Mr. Birkway stared down at the page. It looked

as if he couldn't read the handwriting. He started again.

> *I am very concerned about Mrs., uh, Mrs. Corpse. Her suspicious behavior suggests that she has murdered her own husband—*

Phoebe's eyes blinked rapidly.

"Go on," Ben said. "Finish!"

You could tell that Mr. Birkway was regretting that he had ever started this business with the journals, but all around the room people were shouting, "Yes, finish!" and so he reluctantly continued.

> *I believe she has buried him in her backyard.*

When the bell rang, people went berserk. "Wow! A murder! Who wrote that?" and "Is it real?"

I was out of that room faster than anything, chasing after Phoebe. Megan called out after me, "You kiss *trees?*" I tore out of the building. No Phoebe.

Idiot journals, I thought. Gol-darn idiot journals.

33
THE VISITOR

GRAM AND GRAMPS WERE BOTH STILL AWAKE IN our Frontier Cabin on the edge of Yellowstone National Park. "Aren't you sleepy yet?" I said.

Gram said, "I don't know what's the matter with me. I don't feel like going to sleep at all. I want to know what happened to Peeby."

"I'll tell you about Mr. Birkway's visit. Then I'll stop for tonight."

I went over to Phoebe's after dinner on the day Mr. Birkway had read from my journal about the blackberry kisses and from Phoebe's about Mrs. Cadaver. In Phoebe's bedroom, I said, "I've got two important things to tell you—" The doorbell rang, and we heard a familiar voice.

"That sounds like Mr. Birkway," Phoebe said.

"That's one of the things I want to tell you," I said. "About Mr. Birkway—"

There was a tap on Phoebe's door. Her father

said, "Phoebe? Could you and Sal come downstairs with me?"

I thought Mr. Birkway was going to be mad at Phoebe for what she had written about his sister. The worst thing was that Phoebe didn't even know yet that Mrs. Cadaver was Mr. Birkway's sister. I felt like we were lambs being led to the slaughter. Take us, I thought. Take us and do away with us quickly. We followed Phoebe's father downstairs. There on the sofa was Mr. Birkway, holding Phoebe's journal and looking embarrassed.

"That is my own private journal," Phoebe said. "With my own private thoughts."

"I know," Mr. Birkway said, "and I want to apologize for reading it aloud."

Apologize? That was a relief. It was so quiet in the room that I could hear the leaves being blown off the trees outside.

Mr. Birkway coughed. "I want to explain something," he said. "Mrs. Cadaver is my sister."

"Your sister?" Phoebe said.

"And her husband is dead."

"I thought so," Phoebe said.

"But she didn't murder him," Mr. Birkway said. "Her husband died when a drunk driver rammed into his car. My mother—Mrs. Partridge—was also in the car with Mr. Cadaver. She didn't die, as you know, but she lost her sight."

"Oh—" I said. Phoebe stared at the floor.

"My sister Margaret was the nurse on duty in the emergency room when they brought in her husband and our mother. Margaret's husband died that night."

The whole time Mr. Birkway was talking, Phoebe's father was sitting beside her with his hand resting on her shoulder. It looked like the only thing that was keeping Phoebe from vaporizing into the air and disappearing was his hand resting there.

"I just wanted you to know," Mr. Birkway said, "that Mr. Cadaver is not buried in her backyard. I've also just learned about your mother, Phoebe, and I'm sorry that she's gone, but I assure you that Margaret would not have kidnapped or murdered her."

After Mr. Birkway left, Phoebe and I sat on the front porch. Phoebe said, "If Mrs. Cadaver didn't kidnap or murder my mother, then where *is* she? What can I do? Where should I look?"

"Phoebe," I said. "There's something I've got to tell you."

"Look, Sal, if you're going to tell me she's not

coming back, I don't want to hear it. You might as well go home now."

"I know who the lunatic is. It's Sergeant Bickle's son."

And so we devised a plan.

At home that night, all I could think about was Mrs. Cadaver. I could see her in her white uniform, working in the emergency room. I could see an ambulance pulling up with its blue lights flashing, and her walking briskly to the swinging doors, with her wild hair all around her face. I could see the stretchers being wheeled in, and I could see Mrs. Cadaver looking down at them.

I could feel her heart thumping like mad as she realized it was her own husband and her own mother lying there. I imagined Mrs. Cadaver touching her husband's face. It was as if I was walking in her moccasins, that's how much my own heart was pumping and my own hands were sweating.

I started wondering if the birds of sadness had built their nest in Mrs. Cadaver's hair afterward, and if so, how she got rid of them. Her husband dying and her mother being blinded were events that *would* matter in the course of a lifetime. I saw everyone else going on with their own agendas while Mrs. Cadaver was frantically trying to keep her husband and her mother alive. Did she regret anything? Did she know the worth of water before the well was dry?

All those messages had invaded my brain and affected the way I looked at things.

"Are you sleepy yet, Gram?" I asked. My voice was hoarse from talking so much.

"No, chickabiddy, but you go on to sleep. I'm just going to lie here a while and think about things." She nudged Gramps. "You forgot to say about the marriage bed."

Gramps yawned. "Sorry, gooseberry." He patted the bed and said it.

34
OLD FAITHFUL

THAT NEXT DAY WAS PROBABLY ONE OF THE BEST, and surely the worst, in Gram's and Gramps's lives. The whispers woke me early. It was the sixth day, and the next day was my mother's birthday. We had to get out of Wyoming and through Montana. Gramps was already up, but Gram was lying on the bed, staring at the ceiling. "Did you ever go to sleep?" I asked.

"No," she said, "I didn't feel like sleeping. I can sleep later." She climbed out of bed. "Let's go see that Old Faithful. I've waited my whole entire life to see Old Faithful."

"You've sure got your heart set on that, don't you, you stubborn gooseberry?" said Gramps.

"I sure do," Gram said.

We parked the car and walked up a low hill. I was afraid Gram was going to be disappointed because it didn't look like much at first. There was a rope fence around a mound on the side of the hill. The ground was scrabbly dirt, and in the center of the rope enclosure, about twenty feet away, was a hole.

"Heck," Gram said, "can't we get any closer than this?"

Gramps and I walked over to read a sign about Old Faithful. A park ranger rushed past us yelling, "Ma'am! Ma'am!"

"Gol-dang," Gramps said.

Gram was crawling under the rope. The ranger stopped her. "Ma'am, there's a reason for that rope," he said.

Gram brushed off her dress. "I just wanted a better look."

"Don't worry," the ranger said. "You'll get a good look. Please stay behind the rope."

The sign said that Old Faithful was due to erupt in fifteen minutes. More and more people gathered around the rope. There were people of all ages: little babies crying, grannies sitting on folding stools, teenagers plugged into radio head-sets, couples smooching. There were people speaking languages other than English: next to us was a tour group of Italians; across the way was a group of Germans.

Gram tapped her fingers together, getting more and more excited. "Is it time?" she kept saying. "Is it almost time?"

The crowd became quiet a few minutes before Old Faithful was due to go off. Everyone stared at the hole. Everyone was listening.

"Is it time?" Gram said.

There was a faint noise and a little spit shot out of the hole. The man next to me said, "Aww, is that all—" Another noise, this time a little louder, a grating and crunching sound like walking on gravel. Two fitful spits. "Aww—" the man said.

Then it was like the radiator boiling over or the tea kettle blowing its top. Old Faithful hissed and steamed. A sudden spout of water shot out, maybe three feet high.

"Aww—" the man said. "Is that all—"

More steam, boiling and hissing, and a huge jing-bang spray of water surged out, climbing and climbing, and then more and more, until it looked like a whole river of water was shooting straight up into the air. "It looks like an upsidey-down water-fall!" Gram said. All the while there was a walloping hissing, and I could have sworn the ground rumbled and trembled underneath us. The warm mist blew toward us and people started backing away.

All except Gram. She stood there grinning, tilting her face up to the mist, and staring at that fountain of water. "Oh," she said. "Oh, huzza,

huzza!" She shouted it into the air and noise.

Gramps wasn't watching Old Faithful. He was watching Gram. He put his arms around her and hugged her. "You like this old geyser, don't you?" he said.

"Oh!" Gram said. "Oh yes, I do."

The man next to me was staring open-mouthed at Old Faithful. "Lordy," he said. "Lordy, that's amazing."

Gradually, Old Faithful slowed down. We watched it undo itself and retreat into its hole. We stood there even after everyone else had drifted away. At last Gram sighed and said, "Okay, let's go."

We were inside the car and about to leave when Gram started to cry. "Gol-dang—" Gramps said. "What's the matter?"

Gram sniffled. "Oh nothing. I'm so happy I got to see Old Faithful."

"You old gooseberry," Gramps said, and on we went. "We're gonna eat up Montana," Gramps said. "We're gonna get to the I-dee-ho border tonight. You watch me. I'm putting this pedal to the metal—" He stepped on the gas and peeled out of the parking lot. "I-dee-ho, here we come."

35
THE PLAN

ALL DAY LONG WE ATE UP THE ROAD THROUGH Montana. It hadn't looked so far on the map, but it was all mountains. We started in the foothills of the Rockies as we left Yellowstone, and all day we climbed up and down. Sometimes the road snaked along the side of a cliff, and the only thing between us and the sharp drop was a piddly railing. Often, as we sailed around a bend, we came face to face with a camping trailer swinging its wide body around the curve.

"These roads are a dinger," Gramps said, but he was like a little kid riding a hobby horse. "Gid-yap, let's get a move on," he said, encouraging the car up a hill. "Hee-ya," he said as we swept down the other side.

I felt as if I was torn in two pieces. Half of me was ogling the scenery. I had to admit that it was as pretty as—maybe even prettier than—Bybanks. Trees and rocks and mountains. Rivers and flowers.

Deer and moose and rabbits. It was an amazing country, an enormous country.

But the other half of me was a quivering pile of jelly. I could see our car bursting through the railing and plunging down the cliff. As we approached each curve, I could see us smashing straight on into a truck or a camper. Every time I saw a bus, I watched it sway. I watched its tires spin dangerously close to the gravel at the road's edge. I watched it plunge on, eating up the road, defying those curves.

Gram sat quietly, with her hands folded on her lap. I thought she might sleep, especially after staying awake all night, but she didn't. She wanted to hear about Peeby. So all day long, as I took in the scenery, and as I imagined us in a thousand accidents, and as I prayed underneath it all to any tree whizzing by, I talked about Peeby. I wanted to tell it all today. I wanted to finish it.

On the day after Mr. Birkway appeared at Phoebe's house and told us about Mr. Cadaver, Phoebe and I put our plan in motion. We were going to track down Sergeant Bickle's son and, according to Phoebe, discover the whereabouts of Phoebe's mother. I wasn't positive that Sergeant Bickle's son was a lunatic, and I wasn't convinced he would lead us to Phoebe's mother, but enough of Phoebe's tales had been transplanted into my brain so that I was caught up in the plan. Like Phoebe, I was ready to take some action.

We could hardly sit still all day at school. Phoebe, especially, was fired up. She was worried, too. She was afraid we might not discover her mother alive, and I was beginning to share that fear.

At school, everyone was still buzzing about the journal readings. Everyone wanted to know who had written about the murder. Alex avoided Mary Lou because of what she had said about his being a pink jerk, and Mary Lou avoided Beth Ann because of what Beth Ann had written about the chicken kisses. Megan and Christy taunted Beth Ann with, "Did you really tell Mary Lou that kisses taste like chicken? Did she really believe you?" and they taunted me with, "Do you really kiss *trees*? Didn't you know you're supposed to kiss *boys*?"

In English class, everyone badgered Mr. Birkway to finish reading the journal entry that he had begun yesterday, the one about Mrs. Corpse and the body, but Mr. Birkway did not read any more journals. Instead, he apologized for hurting people's feelings by reading their private thoughts aloud, and he sent us to the library.

There, Ben trailed me. If I looked at the fiction section, he was right beside me. If I moved over to examine the magazines, there he was flipping through one as well. Once, his face made contact with my shoulder. He was definitely trying to plant a kiss on me, I knew he was, but there was nothing I could do about it. I could not help it that whenever he aimed his mouth in my direction, my body was already moving away. I needed a little warning.

I tried remaining completely still for several consecutive minutes, and during those minutes, I detected Ben leaning slightly toward me several times. Each time, however, he drew back, as if someone were controlling him by an invisible thread.

Across the library, Beth Ann called, "Sal, there's a spider—oh, Sal, kill it!"

When the final bell rang, Phoebe and I were out of school like a shot. At Phoebe's house, we examined the telephone directory. "We've got to hurry," Phoebe said, "before Prudence or my father comes home." There were six Bickles listed in the directory. We took turns calling. Each time, we asked for Sergeant Bickle. The first two people said we must have the wrong number. The third number we dialed was busy. The fourth, no answer. The fifth was answered by a crotchety woman who said, "I don't know any sergeants!"

The sixth number was answered by an elderly man who must have been lonely because he talked on and on about once knowing a Sergeant Freeman in the war, but that was back in 1944, and he also knew a Sergeant Bones and a Sergeant Dowdy, but he did not know a Sergeant Bickle.

"What are we going to do?" Phoebe wailed. "Prudence will be home any minute, and we still don't know which is the right Bickle."

The busy number was still busy. The previously unanswered one rang and rang, and just as Phoebe was about to hang up, she heard a voice. "Hello?" she said. "May I speak with Sergeant Bickle, please?" There was a pause as she listened. "He's still at work?" Phoebe was jumping up and down. "Thank you," she said, trying to make her voice serious. "I'll call later. No, no message. Thank you."

"Yes!" she said when she hung up. "Yes, yes, yes!" She was hugging me half to death. "You'll have to do Phase Two. Tonight."

That night, while my father was at Margaret's, I phoned the Bickles. I prayed that Sergeant Bickle wouldn't answer, but I was prepared to disguise my voice in case he did. The phone rang and rang. I hung up. I rehearsed my voice and what I would say. I tried again. On the seventh ring, the phone was answered. It was Sergeant Bickle.

"My name is Susan Longfellow," I said. "I'm a friend of your son's. I was wondering if I might speak with him." I prayed and prayed that he had only one son.

"He isn't here," Sergeant Bickle said. "Would you like to leave a message?"

"Do you know when he'll be home?"

There was a pause. "How did you say you know my son?"

This made me nervous. "How do I know your son? Well, that's a long story—I—basically, the way I know him is—actually, this is a little embarrassing to admit"—my hands were sweating so much I could hardly hang on to the phone—"the library, yes, I know him from the library, and he loaned me a book, but I've lost the book—"

"Maybe you should explain this all to him," Sergeant Bickle said.

"Yes, maybe I should do that."

"I wonder why he gave you this phone number," he said. "I wonder why he didn't give you his number at school."

"At school? Actually, the thing is, I think he did give me that number too, but I've lost it—"

"You sure lose a lot of things," he said. "Would you like his number at school?"

"Yes," I said. "Or better yet, maybe you could give me his address and I'll just send him the book."

"I thought you said you lost the book."

"Actually, yes, but I'm hoping to find it," I said.

"I see," he said. "Just a minute." There was a muffled pause as he put his hand over the receiver and called, "Honey, where's Mike's address?"

Mike! Brilliant! A name! I felt like the Chief Inspector! I felt like I had just discovered the most important clue in the criminal investigation of the century. To top it off, Sergeant Bickle gave me Mike's address. I was sorely tempted to end the conversation by informing Sergeant Bickle that his son was a potential lunatic, but I refrained. I thanked him and immediately phoned Phoebe.

"You're brilliant!" she said. "Tomorrow we'll nail Mike the Lunatic."

36
THE VISIT

THE NEXT DAY, SATURDAY, WHEN PHOEBE AND I reached the bus stop, Ben was standing there. "Oh crud," Phoebe muttered. "Are you waiting for this bus? Are you going to Chanting Falls?"

"Yup," he said.

"To the university?"

"Nope." Ben pushed his hair from his eyes. "There's a hospital there. I'm going to see someone."

"So you're taking this bus," Phoebe said.

"Yes, Free Bee, I am taking this bus. Do you mind?"

The three of us sat on the long bench at the back of the bus. I was in between Phoebe and Ben, and his arm pressed up against mine. Phoebe said we were visiting an old friend, at the university. Each time we rounded a curve, Ben leaned against me or I leaned against him. "Sorry," he said. "Sorry," I said.

At Chanting Falls, we stood on the pavement as the bus roared off. "The university is over there—" Ben pointed down the road. "See ya." And he walked off in the other direction.

"Oh lord," Phoebe said. "Why did Ben have to be on the same bus? It made me very nervous."

It made me nervous too, but for different reasons. Every time I was with him now, my skin tickled and my brain buzzed and my blood romped around as if it were percolating.

The address we had for Mike Bickle was a freshman dormitory. It was a three-story brick building, with hundreds of windows. "Oh no," Phoebe wailed. "I thought it might be a little house or something." Students were coming in and out of the building and walking across the lawn. Some were sitting on the grass or benches studying. In the lobby was a reception desk, with a handsome young man standing behind it. "You do it," Phoebe said. "I just can't."

We stood out like pickles in a pea patch. There were all these grown-up college students and here we were, two puny thirteen-year-old girls. Phoebe said, "I wish I had worn something else." She picked lint off her sweater.

I explained to the man at the desk that I was

looking for my cousin, Mike Bickle. The young man smiled a wide, white smile at me. He checked a roster and said, "You're in the right place. Room 209. You can go on up."

Phoebe nearly choked. "You mean we could go right up to his room?"

"Sure," the young man said. "Through there."

We walked through swinging doors. Phoebe said, "Really, I'm having a heart attack, I know it. I can't do this. Let's get out of here." At the end of the hall, we slipped out the exit. "What if we knocked on his door and he opened it and pulled us inside and slit our throats?"

Students were milling around on the lawn. I looked for an empty bench on which we might sit. On the far side of the lawn I saw the backs of two people, a young man and an older woman. They were holding hands. She turned to him and kissed his cheek.

"Phoebe—" On the bench was Phoebe's mother, and she was kissing the lunatic.

37
A Kiss

PHOEBE WAS STUNNED AND ANGRY, BUT SHE WAS braver than I was. She could watch, but I could not. I assumed that Phoebe would follow me, but I didn't look back. Down the street I tore, trying to remember where the bus stop was. It wasn't until I saw the hospital that I realized I must have missed the bus stop. I ducked inside and was surprised that Phoebe was not behind me.

What I did next was an impulse. A hunch. I asked the hospital receptionist if I could see Mrs. Finney. She flipped through a roster. "Are you a family member?" she said.

"No."

"I'm afraid you can't go up then," she said. "Mrs. Finney is on the psychiatric ward. Family only."

"I was looking for her son. He came here to visit her."

"Maybe they went outside. You could look out back."

Behind the hospital was a wide, sloping lawn, bordered by flower gardens. Scattered across the lawn were benches and chairs, most of them occupied with patients and their visitors. It was a scene much like the one I had just left at the university, except here no one was studying, and some of the people wore dressing gowns.

Ben was sitting cross-legged on the ground in front of a woman in a pink robe. She fidgeted with the sash. Ben saw me and stood up as I crossed the lawn. "This is my mother," he said. I said hello, but she didn't look at me. Instead, she stood and drifted off across the lawn as if we were not there. Ben and I followed.

She reminded me so much of my mother after she returned from the hospital. My mother would stop right in the middle of doing something inside the house and walk out the door. Halfway up the hill, she would sit down to catch her breath. She picked at the grass, got up again, and went a little farther. Sometimes my mother went in the barn and filled the pail with chicken feed, but before she reached the chicken coop, she set the pail down and moved off in another direction. When she could walk farther, my mother rambled over the fields and meadows, in a weaving, snaking pattern, as if she could not make up her mind which way to turn.

We followed Ben's mother back and forth across the lawn, but she never seemed to notice our presence. At last I said I had to go, and that's when it happened.

For one quick moment we both had the same agenda. I looked at him and he looked at me. Both of our heads moved forward. It must have been in slow motion, because I had a split second there to be reminded of Mr. Birkway's drawing of the two heads facing each other, with the vase in between. I wondered, just for an instant, if a vase could fit between us.

If there *had* been a vase, we would have squashed it, because our heads moved completely together and our lips landed in the right place, which was on the other person's lips. It was a real kiss, and it did not taste like chicken.

And then our heads moved slowly backward and we stared out across the lawn, and I felt like the newlY born horse who knows nothing but feels everything.

Ben touched his lips. "Did it taste a little like blackberries to you?" he said.

38
SPIT

AT THIS POINT IN MY STORY, GRAM INTERRUPTED. "Oh yes, yes, yes!" she said. "I've been waiting for that kiss for days. I do like a story with some good kisses in it."

"She's such a gooseberry," Gramps said.

We were churning through Montana. I didn't dare check our progress on the map. I didn't want to discover that we couldn't make it in time. I thought that if I kept talking, and praying underneath, and if we kept moving along those mountainous roads, we had a chance.

Gram said, "But what about Peeby? What about her mother kissing the lunatic? I didn't like that kiss very much. It was the other one I liked—the one with Ben."

I found Phoebe at the bus stop, sitting on the bench. "Where were you?" she asked.

I did not tell her about seeing Ben or his mother. I wanted to, but I couldn't. "I was afraid, Phoebe. I couldn't stay there."

"And I thought you were the brave one," she said. "Oh well, it doesn't matter. Nothing matters. I'm sick of it."

"What happened?"

"Nothing. They sat there on the bench having a gay old time. If I could toss rocks like you can toss rocks, I'd have plonked them both in the back of the head. Did you notice her hair? She's cut it. It's short. And do you know what else she did? In the middle of talking, she leaned over and spit on the grass. Spit! It was disgusting. And the lunatic, do you know what he did when she spit? He *laughed*. Then he leaned over and *he* spit."

"Why would they do that?"

"Who knows? I'm sick of it. My mother can stay there for all I care. She doesn't need me. She doesn't need any of us."

Phoebe was like that all the way home on the bus. She was in an extensively black mood. We got to Phoebe's house just as her father pulled in the driveway. Prudence rushed out of the house saying, "She called, she called, she called! Mom called! She's coming home."

"Terrific," Phoebe muttered.

"What was that, Phoebe?" her father said.

"Nothing."

"She's coming tomorrow," Prudence said. "But—"

"What's wrong?" her father said. "What else did she say?"

"She sounded nervous. She wanted to talk with you—"

"Did she leave a number? I'll call her back—"

"No, she didn't leave any number. She said to tell you not to make any prejudgments."

"What is that supposed to mean?" her father said. "Not make any prejudgments about what?"

"I don't know," Prudence said. "And oh! Most, most, important! She said that she was bringing someone with her."

"That's just grand," Phoebe said. "Just grand."

"Phoebe—?" her father said. "Prudence—did she say who she's bringing?"

"I honestly could not say."

"Did she refer to this person at all? Did she mention a name?" He was getting agitated.

"Why no," Prudence said. "She didn't mention a name. She just said that she was bringing him with her—"

"Him?"

Phoebe looked at me. "Cripes," she said, and she went into the house, slamming the door behind her.

I couldn't believe it. Wasn't she going to tell her father what she had seen? I was bursting at the seams to tell my own father, but when I got home, he and Margaret were sitting on the porch.

Margaret said, "My brother told me you're in his English class. What a surprise." She must have already told my father this, because he didn't look too surprised. "He's a terrific teacher. Do you like him?"

"I suppose." I didn't want to talk about it. I wanted Margaret to vanish.

I had to wait until she went home to tell my father about Phoebe's mother, and when I did tell him, all he said was, "So Mrs. Winterbottom is coming home. That's good." Then he went over to the window and stared out of it for the longest time, and I knew he was thinking about my mother.

All that night I thought about Phoebe and Prudence and Mr. Winterbottom. It seemed like their whole world was going to fall apart the next day when Mrs. Winterbottom walked in all cuddly with the lunatic.

39
HOMECOMING

THE NEXT MORNING, PHOEBE PHONED, BEGGING me to come over. "I can't stand it," she said. "I want a witness."

"For what?"

"I just want a witness."

"Did you tell your father? About your mother and—"

"Are you kidding?" Phoebe said. "You should see him. He and Prudence spent all last night and this morning cleaning the house. They've scrubbed floors and bathrooms, they dusted like fiends, they did laundry and ironing, and they vacuumed. Then they took a good look around. My father said, 'Maybe it looks too good. Your mother will think we can function without her.' So they messed things up. He's very put out with me that I wouldn't help."

I did not want to be a witness to anything, but I felt guilty for running away the day before, and so

I agreed. When I got to her house, Phoebe, Mr. Winterbottom, and Prudence were sitting there staring at each other.

"Didn't she say what time she was coming?" Mr. Winterbottom asked.

Prudence said, "No she did not, and I wish you would quit acting as if it is my fault that she did not say more than she did."

Mr. Winterbottom was a wreck. He jumped up to straighten a pillow, sat back down, and then he leaped up to mess up the pillow again. He went out in the yard and walked around in circles. He changed his shirt twice.

"I hope you don't mind that I'm here," I said.

"Why would I mind?" Mr. Winterbottom said.

Just as I thought they would all go stark raving mad, a taxi pulled up outside. "I can't look," Mr. Winterbottom said, escaping to the kitchen.

"I can't look either," Phoebe said. She followed her father, and I followed Phoebe.

"Well, *gosh*," Prudence said. "I don't know what has gotten into everybody. Aren't you excited to see her?"

From the kitchen, we heard Prudence open the front door. We heard Mrs. Winterbottom say, "Oh sweetie—" Mr. Winterbottom wiped the kitchen counter. We heard Prudence gasp and her mother say, "I'd like you to meet Mike."

"Mike?" Mr. Winterbottom said. He was quite red in the face. I was glad there was no axe in the house or I am fairly certain he would have picked it up and headed straight for Mike.

Phoebe said, "Now, Dad, don't do anything too rash—"

"Mike?" he repeated.

Mrs. Winterbottom called, "George? Phoebe?" We heard her say to Prudence, "Where are they? Didn't you tell them we were coming?"

Mr. Winterbottom took a deep breath. "Phoebe, I'm not sure you or Sal should be around for this."

"Are you kidding?" Phoebe said.

He took another deep breath. "Okay," he said. "Okay. Here we go." He stood up straight and tall and walked through to the living room. Phoebe and I followed.

Honest and truly, I think Phoebe nearly fainted dead away on the carpet. There were two reasons for this. The first one was that Mrs. Winterbottom looked different. Her hair was not only short but also quite stylish. She was wearing lipstick, mascara, and a little blush on her cheeks, and her clothes were altogether unlike anything I had ever seen her in: a white T-shirt, blue jeans, and flat black shoes. Dangling from her ears were thin silver hoop earrings. She looked magnificent, but she did not look like Phoebe's mother.

The second reason that I think Phoebe nearly fainted dead away was that there was Mike Bickle, Phoebe's potential lunatic, in her own living room. It was one thing to *think* he was coming, and another thing to actually see him standing there.

I didn't know what to think. For a second, I thought maybe Mike *had* kidnapped Mrs. Winterbottom and was bringing her back for some ransom money or maybe he was now going to do away with the rest of us. But I kept thinking of seeing them together the day before, and besides, Mrs. Winterbottom looked too terrific to have been held captive. She did look frightened, but not of Mike. She seemed afraid of her husband.

"Dad," Phoebe whispered, "that's the lunatic."

"Oh Phoebe," her mother said, pressing her fingers to her cheek, and when she made that familiar gesture, Phoebe looked as if her heart was splitting into a thousand pieces. Mrs. Winterbottom hugged Phoebe, but Phoebe did not hug her back.

Mr. Winterbottom said, "Norma, I hope you are going to explain exactly what is going on here." He was trying to make his voice firm, but it trembled.

Prudence stared at Mike. She seemed to find him handsome and was flirting with him. She fluffed her hair away from her neck.

Mrs. Winterbottom tried to put her arms around Mr. Winterbottom, but he pulled away. "I think we deserve an explanation," he said. He, too, stared at Mike.

Was she in love with Mike? He seemed awfully, awfully young—not much older than Prudence.

Mrs. Winterbottom sat down on the sofa and began to cry. It was a terrible, terrible moment. It was hard to make any sense out of what she said at first. She was talking about being respectable and how maybe Mr. Winterbottom would never forgive her, but she was tired of being so respectable. She had tried very, very hard all these years to be perfect, but she had to admit she was quite unperfect. She said there was something that she had never told her husband, and she feared he would not forgive her for it.

Mr. Winterbottom's hands trembled. He did not say anything. Mrs. Winterbottom motioned for Mike to join her on the sofa. Mr. Winterbottom cleared his throat several times, but still he said nothing.

Mrs. Winterbottom said, "Mike is my son."

Mr. Winterbottom, Prudence, Phoebe, and I all said, "Your *son*?"

Mrs. Winterbottom stared at her husband. "George, I know you will think I am not—or was not—respectable, but it was before I met you, and I had to give him up for adoption and I could hardly bear to think of it and—"

Mr. Winterbottom said, "Respectable? Respectable? The hell with respectable!" Mr. Winterbottom did not normally swear.

Mrs. Winterbottom stood up. "Mike found *me*, and at first I was frightened of what that would mean. I've lived such a tiny life—"

Phoebe took her father's hand.

"—and I had to go away and sort things out. I haven't yet met Mike's adoptive parents, but Mike and I have spent a lot of time talking, and I've been thinking—"

Mike looked down at his feet.

"Are you going to leave?" Mr. Winterbottom asked.

Mrs. Winterbottom looked as if he had slapped her. "Leave?"

"Again, I mean," Mr. Winterbottom said.

"Only if you want me to," she said. "Only if you

cannot live with such an unrespectable—"

"I said to hell with respectable!" Mr. Winterbottom said. "What's all this about respectable? It's not respectable I'm concerned about. I'm more concerned that you couldn't—or wouldn't—tell me about any of this."

Mike stood up. "I knew it wouldn't work," he said.

Mr. Winterbottom said, "I have nothing against you, Mike—I just don't know you." He looked at his wife. "I don't think I know you, either."

I was wishing I was invisible. Outside, the leaves were falling to the ground, and I was infinitely sad, sad down to my bones. I was sad for Phoebe and her parents and Prudence and Mike, sad for the leaves that were dying, and sad for myself, for something I had lost.

I saw Mrs. Partridge through the window, standing on Phoebe's front walk.

Mr. Winterbottom said, "I think we all need to sit down and talk. Maybe we can sort something out." Then he did what I think was a noble thing. He went over to Mike and shook his hand and said, "I did always think a son would be a nice addition to this family."

Mrs. Winterbottom looked relieved. Prudence

smiled at Mike. Phoebe stood motionless, off to the side.

"I'd better go," I said.

Everyone turned to me as if I had just dropped through the roof. Mr. Winterbottom said, "Sal, I'm sorry, I truly am." To Mike, he said, "Sal is like another member of the family."

Mrs. Winterbottom said, "You're mad at me, aren't you, Phoebe?"

"Yes," Phoebe said. "I most certainly am." Phoebe took my sleeve and pulled me toward the door. "When you all decide exactly how many people are in this family, let me know."

We stepped out on the porch just as Mrs. Partridge placed a white envelope on the steps.

40
THE GIFTS

IT SEEMED FITTING THAT AT THIS POINT IN MY STORY of Phoebe, Gramps called out, "I-dee-ho!" We were high in the mountains and had just crossed the Montana border into Idaho. For the first time, I believed we were going to make it to Lewiston by the next day, the twentieth of August, my mother's birthday.

Gramps suggested we press on to Coeur d'Alene, about an hour away, where we could spend the night. From there, Lewiston was about a hundred miles due south, an easy morning's journey. "How does that sound to you, gooseberry?" Gram was still, her head pressed against the back of the seat and her hands folded in her lap. "Gooseberry?"

When Gram spoke, you could hear the rattle in her chest. "Oh, that's fine," she said.

"Gooseberry, are you feeling okay?"

"I'm a little tired," she said.

"We'll get you to a bed real soon." Gramps glanced back at me, troubled.

"Gram, if you want to stop now, that would be okay," I said.

"Oh no," she said. "I'd like to sleep in Coeur d'Alene tonight. Your momma sent us a postcard from Coeur d'Alene, and on it was a bountiful blue lake." She coughed a long, rattly cough.

Gramps said, "Okay then, bountiful blue lake, here we come."

Gram said, "I'm so glad Peeby's momma came home. I wish your momma could come home too."

Gramps nodded his head for about five minutes. Then he handed me a tissue and said, "Tell us about Mrs. Partridge. What was she doing leaving a gol-dang envelope on Peeby's porch?"

That's what Phoebe and I wanted to know. "Did you want something, Mrs. Partridge?" I asked.

She put her hand to her lips. "Hmm," she said.

Phoebe snatched the envelope and ripped it open. She read the message aloud: "Don't judge a man until you've walked two moons in his moccasins."

Mrs. Partridge turned to go. "Bye-bye," she said.

"Mrs. Partridge," Phoebe called. "We've already had this one."

"I beg your pardon?" Mrs. Partridge said.

"It was you, wasn't it?" Phoebe said. "You've been creeping around leaving these things, haven't you?"

"Did you like them?" Mrs. Partridge said. As she stood there in the middle of the sidewalk, with her head tilted up at us, and that quizzical look on her face, she looked like a mischievous child. "Margaret reads them to me from the paper each day, and when there's a nice one, I ask her to copy it down. I'm sorry I gave you that one about the moccasins already. My noggin forgot."

"But why did you bring them *here*?" Phoebe said.

"I thought they would be grandiful surprises for you—like fortune cookies, only I didn't have any cookies to put them in. Did you like them anyway?"

Phoebe looked at me for a long minute. Then she went down the steps and said, "Mrs. Partridge, when was it you met my brother?"

"You said you didn't have a brother," Mrs. Partridge said.

"I know, but you said you met him. When was that?"

She tapped her head. "Noggin, remember. Let's see. Some time ago. A week? Two weeks? He came to my house by mistake. He let me feel his face. That's why I thought he was your brother. He has a similar face. Isn't that peculible?"

Phoebe said, "No more peculible than most things lately." As Mrs. Partridge tottered back to her house, Phoebe said, "It's a peculible world, Sal." She walked across the grass and spit into the street. She said, "Come on, try it." I spit into the street. "What do you think?" Phoebe said. We spit again.

It might sound disgusting, but to tell the truth, we got a great deal of pleasure from those spits. I doubt if I ever could explain why that was, but for some reason it seemed the perfect thing to do, and when Phoebe turned around and went into the house, I knew that was the right thing for her to do too.

With the courage of that spit in me, I went to see Margaret Cadaver, and we had a long talk, and that's when I found out how she met my father. It was painful to talk with her, and I even cried in front of her, but afterward I understood why my father liked to be with her.

Ben was sitting on my front steps when I got home. He said, "I brought you something. It's out back." He led me around the side of the house and there, strutting across that little patch of grass, was a chicken.

I was never in my life so happy to see a chicken.

Ben said, "I named it, but you can change the name if you want."

When I asked him what its name was, he leaned forward, and I leaned forward and another kiss happened, a spectacular kiss, a perfect kiss, and Ben said, "Its name is Blackberry."

"Oh," Gram said, "is that the end of the Peeby story?"

"Yes," I said. That wasn't quite true, I suppose, as I could have told more. I could have told about Phoebe getting adjusted to having a brother, and to her "new" mother, and all of that, but that part was still going on, even as we traveled through the mountains. It was a whole different story.

"I liked that story about Peeby, and I'm glad it wasn't too awfully sad."

Gram closed her eyes and for the next hour as Gramps drove toward Coeur d'Alene, he and I listened to her rattly breathing. I watched her lying there so still, so calm. "Gramps," I whispered. "She looks a little gray, doesn't she?"

"Yes she does, chickabiddy, yes she does." He stepped on the gas and we raced toward Coeur d'Alene.

41
THE OVERLOOK

AT COEUR D'ALENE, WE WENT STRAIGHT TO THE hospital. Gramps had tried to wake Gram when he saw the lake. "Gooseberry?" Gramps said. She slumped sideways on the seat. "Gooseberry?"

The doctors said Gram had had a stroke. Gramps insisted on being with her while she underwent tests, though an intern had tried to dissuade him. "She's unconscious," the intern said. "She won't know whether you're here or not."

"Sonny, I've been by her side for fifty-one years, except for three days when she left me for the egg man. I'm holding on to her hand, see? If you want me to let go, you'll have to chop my hand off."

They let him stay with her. While I was waiting in the lobby, a man came in with an old beagle. The receptionist told him he would have to leave the dog outside. "By herself?" the man said.

I said, "I'll watch her. I had a dog just like her once." I took the old beagle outside, and when I sat down on the grass, the beagle put her head in my lap and murmured in that special way dogs have. Gramps calls it a dog's purr.

I wondered if Gram's snake bite had anything to do with her stroke, and if Gramps felt guilty for whizzing off the highway and stopping at that river. If we hadn't gone to that river, Gram would never have been bitten by that snake. And then I started thinking about my mother's stillborn baby and maybe if I hadn't climbed that tree and if my mother hadn't carried me, maybe the baby would have lived and my mother never would have gone away, and everything would still be as it used to be.

But as I sat there thinking these things, it occurred to me that a person couldn't stay all locked up in the house like Phoebe and her mother had tried to do at first. A person had to go out and do things and see things, and I wondered, for the first time, if this had something to do with Gram and Gramps taking me on this trip.

The beagle in my lap was just like our Moody Blue. I rubbed her head and prayed for Gram. I thought about Moody Blue's litter of puppies. For the first week, Moody Blue wouldn't let anyone come anywhere near those puppies. She licked them clean and nuzzled them. They squealed and pawed their way up to her with their eyes still sealed.

Gradually, Moody Blue let us touch the puppies, but she kept her sharp eyes on us, and if we tried to take a puppy out of her sight, she growled. Within a few weeks, the puppies were stumbling away from her, and Moody Blue spent her days herding them back, but when they were about six weeks old, Moody Blue started ignoring them. She snapped at them and pushed them away. I told my mother that Moody Blue was being terrible. "She hates her puppies."

"It's not terrible," my mother said. "It's normal. She's weaning them from her."

"Does she have to do that? Why can't they stay with her?"

"It isn't good for her or for them. They have to become independent. What if something happened to Moody Blue? They wouldn't know how to survive without her."

While I prayed for Gram outside the hospital, I wondered if my mother's trip to Idaho was like Moody Blue's behavior. Maybe part of it was for my mother and part of it was for me.

When the beagle's owner returned, I went back inside. It was after midnight when a nurse told me I could see Gram. She was lying, still and gray, on the bed. A little dribble was coming out of one side of her mouth. Gramps was leaning over her, whispering in her ear. A nurse said, "I don't think she can hear you."

"Of course she can hear me," Gramps said. "She'll always be able to hear me."

Gram's eyes were closed. Wires were attached to her chest and to a monitor, and a tube was taped to her hand. I wanted to hold her and wake her up. Gramps said, "We're gonna be here a while, chickabiddy." He reached in his pocket and pulled out his car keys. "Here, in case you need anything from the car." He handed me a crumpled wad of money. "In case you need it."

"I don't want to leave Gram," I said.

"Heck," he said. "She doesn't want you sitting around this old hospital. You just whisper in her ear if you want to tell her anything, and then you go do what you have to do. We're not going anywhere, your grandmother and I. We'll be right here." He winked at me. "You be careful, chickabiddy."

I leaned over and whispered in Gram's ear and

then I left. In the car, I studied the map, leaned back in the seat, and closed my eyes. Gramps knew what I was going to do.

The key was cold in my hand. I studied the map again. One curvy road ran direct from Coeur d'Alene to Lewiston. I started the car, backed it up, drove around the parking lot, stopped, and turned off the engine. I counted the money in my pocket and looked at the map once more.

In the course of a lifetime, there were some things that mattered.

Although I was terrified when I drove out of the parking lot, once I was on the highway, I felt better. I drove slowly, and I knew how to do it. I prayed to every passing tree, and there were a thumping lot of trees along the way.

It was a narrow, winding road, without traffic. It took me four hours to drive the hundred miles from Coeur d'Alene to the top of Lewiston Hill— which, to me, was more of a mountain than a hill. I pulled into the overlook at the top. In the valley far below was Lewiston, with the Snake River winding through it. Between me and Lewiston was the treacherous road with its hairpin turns that twisted back and forth down the mountain.

I peered over the rail, looking for the bus that I

knew was still somewhere down there on the side of the mountain, but I couldn't see it. "I can do this," I said to myself over and over. "I can do this."

I eased the car back onto the road. At the first curve, my heart started thumping. My palms were sweating and slippery on the wheel. I crept along with my foot on the brake, but the road doubled back so sharply and plunged so steeply that even with my foot on the brake, the car was going faster than I wanted it to. When I came out of that curve, I was in the outside lane, the one nearest to the side of the cliff. It was a sharp drop down, with only a thin cable strung between occasional posts to mark the edge of the road.

Back and forth across the hill the road snaked. For a half mile, I was on the inside against the hill and felt safer, and then I came to one of those awful curves, and for the next half mile I was on the outside, and the dark slide of the hillside stretched down, down, down. Back and forth I went: a half mile safe, a curve, a half mile edging the side of the cliff.

Halfway down was another overlook, a thin extra lane marked off less as an opportunity to gaze at the scenery, I thought, than to allow drivers a chance to stop and gather their wits. I wondered how many people had abandoned their cars at this point and walked the remaining miles down. As I stood looking over the side, another car pulled into the overlook. A man got out and stood near me, smoking a cigarette. "Where are the others?" he asked.

"What others?"

"Whoever's with you. Whoever's driving."

"Oh," I said. "Around—"

"Taking a pee, eh?" he said, referring, I gathered, to whoever was supposedly with me. "A helluva road to be driving at night, isn't it? I do it every night. I work up in Pullman and live down there—" He pointed to the lights of Lewiston and the black river. "You been here before?" he said.

"No."

"See that?" He indicated a spot somewhere below.

I peered into the darkness. Then I saw the severed treetops and the rough path cut through the brush. At the end of this path I could see something shiny and metallic reflecting the moonlight. It was the one thing I had been looking for.

"A bus went off the road here—a year or more ago," he said. "Skidded right there, coming out of that last turn, and went sliding into this here overlook and on through the railing and rolled over and over into those trees. A helluva thing. When I came home that night, rescuers were still hacking their way through the brush to get to it. Only one person survived, ya know?"

I knew.

42
THE BUS AND THE WILLOW

WHEN THE MAN DROVE OFF, I CRAWLED BENEATH the railing and made my way down the hill toward the bus. In the east the sky was smoky gray, and I was glad for the approaching dawn. In the year and a half since the trail was hacked out, the brush had begun to grow back. Wet with dew, straggly branches slapped and scratched at my legs and hid uneven ground so that several times I tripped, tumbling and sliding downward.

The bus lay on its side like an old sick horse, its broken headlights staring out mournfully into the surrounding trees. Most of the huge rubber tires were punctured and grotesquely twisted on their axles. I climbed up onto the bus's side, hoping to make my way down to an open window, but there were two enormous gashes torn into the side, and the jagged metal was peeled back like a sardine tin. Through a smashed window behind the driver's seat, I saw a jumbled mess of twisted seats and chunks of foam rubber. Everything was dusted over with fuzzy, green mold.

I had imagined that I would drop through a window and walk down the aisle, but there was no space inside to move. I had wanted to scour every inch of the bus, looking for something—anything—that might be familiar.

By now the sky was pale pink, and it was easier to find the uphill trail, but harder going as it was a steep incline. By the time I reached the top, I was muddy and scratched from head to toe. It wasn't until I had crawled beneath the railing that I noticed the car parked behind Gramps's red Chevrolet.

It was the sheriff. He was talking on his radio when he saw me, and he motioned for his deputy to get out. The deputy said, "We were just about to come down there after you. We saw you up on top of the bus. You kids ought to know better. What were you doing down there at this time of day, anyway?"

Before I could answer, the sheriff climbed out of his car. He settled his hat on his head and shifted his holster. "Where are the others?" he said.

"There aren't any others," I said.

"Who brought you up here?"

"I brought myself."

"Whose car is this?"

"My grandfather's."

"And where is he?" The sheriff glanced to left and right, as if Gramps might be hiding in the bushes.

"He's in Coeur d'Alene."

The sheriff said, "Pardon?"

So I told him about Gram and about how Gramps had to stay with her and about how I had driven from Coeur d'Alene *very carefully.*

The sheriff said, "Now let me get this straight," and he repeated everything I said, ending with, "and you're telling me that you drove from Coeur d'Alene to this spot on this hill all by yourself?"

"Very carefully," I said. "My gramps taught me how to drive, and he taught me to drive very carefully."

The sheriff said to the deputy, "I am afraid to ask this young lady exactly how old she is. Why don't you ask her?"

The deputy said, "How old are you?" I told him. The sheriff gave me a stern look and said, "I don't suppose you would mind telling me exactly what was so all-fired important that you couldn't wait for someone with a legitimate driver's license to bring you to the fair city of Lewiston?"

And so I told him all the rest. When I had finished, he returned to his car and talked into his radio some more. Then he told me to get in his car and he told the deputy to follow in Gramps's car. I thought the sheriff was probably going to put me in jail, and it wasn't the thought of jail that bothered me so much. It was knowing that I was this close and might not be able to do what I had come to do, and it was knowing that I needed to get back to Gram.

He did not take me to jail, however. He drove across the bridge into Lewiston and on through the city and up a hill. He drove into Longwood, stopped at the caretaker's house, and went inside. Behind us was the deputy in Gramps's car. The caretaker came out and pointed off to the right, and the sheriff got back in the car and drove off in that direction.

It was a pleasant place. The Snake River curved behind this section, and tall, full-leaved trees grew here and there across the lawn. The sheriff parked the car and led me up a path toward the river, and there, on a little hill overlooking the river and the valley, was my mother's grave.

On the tombstone, beneath her name and the dates of her birth and death, was an engraving of a maple tree, and it was only then, when I saw the stone and her name—Chanhassen "Sugar" Pickford Hiddle—and the engraving of the tree, that I knew, by myself and for myself, that she was not coming back. I asked if I could sit there for a little while, because I wanted to memorize the place. I wanted to memorize the grass and the trees, the smells and the sounds.

In the midst of the still morning, with only the sound of the river gurgling by, I heard a bird. It was singing a birdsong, a true, sweet birdsong. I looked all around and then up into the willow that leaned toward the river. The birdsong came from the top of the willow and I did not want to look too closely, because I wanted it to be the tree that was singing.

I kissed the willow. "Happy birthday," I said.

In the sheriff's car, I said, "She isn't actually gone at all. She's singing in the trees."

"Whatever you say, Miss Salamanca Hiddle."

"You can take me to jail now."

43
OUR GOOSEBERRY

INSTEAD OF TAKING ME TO JAIL, THE SHERIFF DROVE me to Coeur d'Alene, with the deputy following us in Gramps's car. The sheriff gave me a lengthy and severe lecture about driving without a license, and he made me promise that I would not drive again until I was sixteen.

"Not even on Gramps's farm?" I said.

He looked straight ahead at the road. "I suppose people are going to do whatever they want to on their own farms," he said, "as long as they have a lot of room to maneuver and as long as they are not endangering the lives of any other persons or animals. But I'm not saying you ought to. I'm not giving you permission or anything."

I asked him to tell me about the bus accident. When I asked him if he had been there that night and if he had seen anyone brought out of the bus, he said, "You don't want to know all that. A person shouldn't have to think about those things."

"Did you see my mother?"

"I saw a lot of people, Salamanca, and maybe I saw your mother and maybe I didn't, but I'm sorry to say that if I did see her, I didn't know it. I remember your father coming in to the station. I do remember that, but I wasn't with him when—I wasn't there when—"

"Did you see Mrs. Cadaver?" I said.

"How do you know about Mrs. Cadaver?" he said. "Of course I saw Mrs. Cadaver. Everyone saw Mrs. Cadaver. Nine hours after that bus rolled over, as all those stretchers were being carried up the hill, and everyone despairing—there was her hand coming up out of the window and everyone was shouting because there it was, a moving hand." He glanced at me. "I wish it had been your mother's hand."

"Mrs. Cadaver was sitting next to my mother," I said.

"Oh."

"They were strangers to each other when they got on that bus, but by the time they got off, six days later, they were friends. My mother told Mrs. Cadaver all about me and my father and our farm in Bybanks. She told Mrs. Cadaver about the fields and the blackberries and Moody Blue and the chickens and the singing tree. I think that if she told Mrs. Cadaver all that, then my mother must have been missing us, don't you think?"

"I'm sure of it," the sheriff said. "And how do you know all this?"

So I explained to him how Mrs. Cadaver had told me all this on the day Phoebe's mother returned. Mrs. Cadaver told me about how my father visited her in the hospital in Lewiston after he had buried my mother. He came to see the only survivor from the bus crash, and when he learned that Mrs. Cadaver had been sitting next to my mother, they started talking about her. They talked for six hours.

Mrs. Cadaver told me about her and my father writing to each other, and about how my father needed to get away from Bybanks for a while. I asked Mrs. Cadaver why my father hadn't told me how he had met her, and she said he had tried, but I didn't want to hear it, and he didn't want to upset me. He thought I might dislike Margaret because she had survived and my mother had not.

"Do you love him?" I had asked Mrs. Cadaver. "Are you going to marry him?"

"Goodness!" she said. "It's a little early for that. He's holding on to me because I was with your mother and held her hand in her last moments.

Your father isn't ready to love anyone else yet. Your mother was one of a kind."

That's true. She was.

And even though Mrs. Cadaver had told me all this and had told me how she had been with my mother in her last minutes, I still did not believe that my mother was actually dead. I still thought that there might have been a mistake. I don't know what I had hoped to find in Lewiston. Maybe I expected that I would see her walking through a field and I would call to her and she would say, "Oh Salamanca, my left arm," and "Oh Salamanca, take me home."

I slept for the last fifty miles into Coeur d'Alene and when I awoke, I was sitting in the sheriff's car outside the hospital entrance. The sheriff was coming out of the hospital. He handed me an envelope and slid in beside me on the seat.

In the envelope was a note from Gramps giving the name of the motel he was staying at. Beneath that he had written, "I am sorry to say that our gooseberry died at three o'clock this morning."

Gramps was sitting on the side of the bed in the motel, talking on the telephone. When he saw me and the sheriff at the door, he put the phone down and hugged me to him. The sheriff told Gramps how sorry he was and that he didn't think it was the time or place to give anybody a lecture about un-derage granddaughters driving down a mountain-side in the middle of the night. He handed Gramps his car key and asked Gramps if he needed help making any arrangements.

Gramps said he had taken care of most things. Gram's body was being flown back to Bybanks, where my father would meet the plane. Gramps and I were going to finish what had to be done in Coeur d'Alene and leave the next morning.

After the sheriff and his deputy left, I noticed Gram's and Gramps's open suitcase. Inside were Gram's things, all mixed in with Gramps's clothes. I picked up her baby powder and smelled it. On the desk was a crumpled letter. When Gramps saw me look at it, he said, "I wrote her a letter last night. It's a love letter."

Gramps lay down on the bed and stared up at the ceiling. "Chickabiddy," he said, "I miss my gooseberry." He put one arm over his eyes. His other hand patted the empty space beside him. "This ain't—" he said. "This ain't—"

"It's okay," I said. I sat down on the other side of the bed and held his hand. "This ain't your mar-riage bed."

About five minutes later, Gramps cleared his throat and said, "But it will have to do."

44
BYBANKS

WE'RE BACK IN BYBANKS NOW. MY FATHER AND I are living on our farm again, and Gramps is living with us. Gram is buried in the aspen grove where she and Gramps were married. We miss our gooseberry every single day.

Lately, I've been wondering if there might be something hidden behind the fireplace, because just as the fireplace was behind the plaster wall and my mother's story was behind Phoebe's, I think there was a third story behind Phoebe's and my mother's, and that was about Gram and Gramps.

On the day after Gram was buried, her friend Gloria—the one Gram thought was so much like Phoebe, and the one who had a hankering for Gramps—came to visit Gramps. They sat on our porch while Gramps talked about Gram for four hours straight. Gloria asked if we had any aspirin. She had a grand headache. We haven't seen her since.

I wrote to Tom Fleet, the boy who helped Gram when the snake took a snack out of her leg. I told him that Gram made it back to Bybanks, but unfortunately she came in a coffin. I described the aspen grove where she was buried and told him about the river nearby. He wrote back, saying that he was sorry about Gram and maybe he would come and visit that aspen grove someday. Then he asked, "Is your riverbank private property?"

Gramps is giving me more driving lessons in the pickup truck. We practice over on Gramps's old farm, where the new owner lets us clonk around on the dirt roads. With us rides Gramps's new beagle puppy, which he named Huzza Huzza. Gramps pets the puppy and smokes his pipe as I drive, and we both play the moccasin game. It's a game we made up on our way back from Idaho. We take turns pretending we are walking in someone else's moccasins.

"If I were walking in Peeby's moccasins, I would be jealous of a new brother dropping out of the sky."

"If I were in Gram's moccasins right this minute, I would want to cool my feet in that river over there."

"If I were walking in Ben's moccasins, I would

miss Salamanca Hiddle."

On and on we go. We walk in everybody's moccasins, and we have discovered some interesting things that way. One day I realized that our whole trip out to Lewiston had been a gift from Gram and Gramps to me. They were giving me a chance to walk in my mother's moccasins—to see what she had seen and feel what she might have felt on her last trip.

I also realized that there were good reasons why my father didn't take me to Idaho when he got the news of her death. He was too grief-stricken, and he was trying to spare me. Only later did he understand that I had to go and see for myself. He was right about one thing, though: we didn't need to bring her body back because she *is* in the trees, the barn, the fields. Gramps is different. He needs Gram right here. He needs to walk out to that aspen grove to see his gooseberry.

One afternoon, after we had been talking about Prometheus stealing fire from the sun to give to man, and about Pandora opening up the forbidden box with all the evils of the world in it, Gramps said that those myths evolved because people needed a way to explain where fire came from and why there was evil in the world. That made me think of Phoebe and the lunatic, and I said, "If I were walking in Phoebe's moccasins, I would have to believe in a lunatic and an axe-wielding Mrs. Cadaver to explain my mother's disappearance."

Phoebe and her family helped me, I think. They helped me to think about and understand my own mother. Phoebe's tales were like my fishing in the air: for a while I needed to believe that my mother was not dead and that she would come back.

I still fish in the air sometimes.

It seems to me that we can't explain all the truly awful things in the world like war and murder and brain tumors, and we can't fix these things, so we look at the frightening things that are closer to us and we magnify them until they burst open. Inside is something that we can manage, something that isn't as awful as it had at first seemed. It is a relief to discover that although there might be axe murderers and kidnappers in the world, most people seem a lot like us: sometimes afraid and sometimes brave, sometimes cruel and sometimes kind.

I decided that bravery is looking Pandora's box full in the eye as best you can, and then turning to the other box, the one with the smoothbeautiful folds inside: Momma kissing trees, my Gram saying, "Huzza, huzza," Gramps and his marriage bed.

My mother's postcards and her hair are still beneath the floorboards in my room. I reread all the postcards when I came home. Gram and Gramps and I had been to every place my mother had. There are the Black Hills, Mt. Rushmore, the Badlands—the only card that is still hard for me to read is the one from Coeur d'Alene, the one that I received two days after she died.

When I drive Gramps around in his truck, I also tell him all the stories my mother told me. His favorite is a Navaho one about Estsanatlehi. She's a woman who never dies. She grows from baby to mother to old woman and then turns into a baby again, and on and on she goes, living a thousand, thousand lives. Gramps likes this, and so do I.

I still climb the sugar maple tree, and I have heard the singing tree sing. The sugar maple tree is my thinking place. Yesterday in the sugar maple, I realized that I was jealous of three things.

The first jealousy is a foolish one. I am jealous of whoever Ben wrote about in his journal, because it was not me.

The second jealousy is this: I am jealous that my mother had wanted more children. Wasn't I enough? When I walk in her moccasins, though, I say, "If I were my mother, I might want more children—not because I don't love my Salamanca, but because I love her so much. I want more of these." Maybe that is a fish in the air and maybe it isn't, but it is what I want to believe.

The last jealousy is not foolish, nor is it one that will go away just yet. I am still jealous that Phoebe's mother came back and mine did not.

I miss my mother.

Ben and Phoebe write to me all the time. Ben sent me a valentine in the middle of October that said,

> *Roses are red,*
> *Dirt is brown,*
> *Please be my valentine,*
> *Or else I'll frown.*

There was a P.S. added: *I've never written poetry before.*

I sent a valentine back that said:

> *Dry is the desert,*
> *Wet is the rain,*
> *Your love for me*
> *Is not in vain.*

I added a P.S. that said, *I've never written any poetry either.*

Ben and Phoebe and Mrs. Cadaver and Mrs. Partridge are all coming to visit next month. There is a chance that Mr. Birkway might come as well, but Phoebe hopes not, as she does not think she could stand to be in a car for that long with a teacher. My father and I have been scrubbing the house for their visit. I can't wait to show Phoebe and Ben the swimming hole and the fields, the hayloft and the trees, and the cows and the chickens. Blackberry, the chicken that Ben gave me, is queen of the coop, and I'll show Ben her, too. I am hoping, also, for some blackberry kisses.

But for now, Gramps has his beagle, and I have a chicken and a singing tree, and that's the way it is.

Huzza, huzza.

))